T0374455

A Date
with
Destiny

CAROLYN J. POLLACK

ISBN: 978-1-4907-0966-6 (sc)
ISBN: 978-1-4907-0965-9 (e)

Trafford rev. 06/26/2014

www.trafford.com

North America & international
toll-free: 1 888 232 4444 (USA & Canada)
fax: 812 355 4082

A Date
with
Destiny

ACKNOWLEDGEMENTS

||||||||||||||||||||||||||||

I would like to acknowledge a very special thank you to one of my work friends. Elizabeth (Lizzy) Geer has graciously agreed to pose for the cover of A Date With Destiny to portray the character of Tarmin Elizabeth Blain.

Also, I would like to say a very heartfelt thank you to Karen Alice Ebert who has once again come to my aid and taken some fantastic photos for the front and back cover.

CHAPTER ONE

||||||||||||||||||||||||||||

Zac read through the pile of applications which were splayed out haphazardly before him on his desk. He was annoyed that he had to be here in his office at all. His aunt, he knew, could have taken care of this stuff standing on her head. Interviewing job applicants was a standard and straight forward procedure, one that she'd carried out for him numerous times before. So why call him in today of all days.

He couldn't understand why he'd been pulled off the golf course to come into work on the only day he'd had off in weeks to conduct mundane job interviews. He employed people to do this kind of thing. It was one of the few remaining perks left being head of your own company.

Heads will roll, he thought sourly to himself as he buzzed through to his secretary asking her less than politely to send in the next applicant, then on an impulse born out of his desperation to be back on the golf course he buzzed again telling her not to worry, he'd chosen the successful applicant. She could dismiss anyone who happened to be out there.

"Eenie, meenie, miney, moe," he said as his hand rotated slowly above the pile of job applications he had on his desk before he randomly reached down into the pile and extracted one.

"There," he said with satisfaction, "all done." If he hurried he'd still be able to play the last nine holes.

Glancing down at the application he'd chosen, he briefly examined the information it contained.

"Ms. Tarmin Elizabeth Blain; age 25; single," he stated to himself matter-of-factly emphasising the Ms. giving the word a slightly elongated sound. It amused him the way single women today abbreviated their title. It didn't make them any less single or any more qualified, so why do it in the first place. He flipped through the pages looking for the photograph, he always asked for a photograph.

The face that looked unblinkingly back at him was very unpretentious. The owner of that face hadn't bothered with fundamental things like make-up or a flattering hairstyle and he could plainly detect a fine smattering of chestnut freckles which stretched across the bridge of her petite nose before fanning out across her high cheekbones to finally peter out somewhere near her temples. He couldn't readily see the colour of her eyes for they were hidden behind thick ugly glasses which did nothing to flatter the contours of her face. If he had to hazard a guess as to their colour, he'd have said they were a very dark blue which was unusual for her hair was a rich chestnut colour, the same as her freckles he observed absently. Most striking, but the rich locks were pulled severely back from her face; *probably in a bun,* he thought disdainfully suppressing a slight shudder. The style brought back vivid memories of his misspent school days and of one teacher in particular. He'd always had to report to her when he'd been in trouble which hadn't been often to be sure, but she'd always been less than sympathetic not wanting to listen to his carefully orchestrated explanations. He quickly brought his mind back to the woman in the photograph not wanting to waste any more unnecessary time on thoughts concerning the misadventures of his schooldays.

She wore a tan coat, which was completely wrong for her, unflatteringly so. He surmised it was probably part of a tailored suit that did absolutely nothing for her colouring making her flawless complexion look wan and uninviting. Her mouth looked equally uninviting, although full and luscious looking even without lip-gloss. It was set firmly in a straight line, showing not a hint of a smile and he wondered what someone would have to do to bring a pleasurable smile to that uncompromising mouth. If she was to stick the tip of her tongue out just by the smallest fraction and maybe relax those lips, letting them smile, really smile, a full 'I'm in love with the whole world' kind of smile, he was sure that 'plain Jane' rigidly set face would be transformed into a beautiful Grecian goddess full of soft, flowing vibrant life.

He didn't go for the Grecian goddess type himself, but he did like his women to make the most of their god given attributes. *Why not?* There was nothing more appealing to a man than a woman who knew how to please the opposite sex. He made no apology for his sexist point of view. He enjoyed looking, touching too. He made a mental note reminding himself that he'd have to call Colleen to tell her about the tickets he'd been able to pick up for next week's theatre performance. They were a parting gesture on his part. The relationship was going nowhere. He'd never thought of sex as a duty, but lately with Colleen he felt more like a trained performer rather than an experienced lover. Once this happened it was time to get out.

Now where was I, he thought once more bringing his mind back to the task at hand, *oh yes, plain Jane,* and the fact that he found great pleasure in sampling the feminine smorgasbord from which he was able to choose on a regular basis. He didn't think he was conceited, far from it, but if women were going to flaunt their bodies at him, who was he to deny them the pleasure of his in return, it only seemed fair? To date he'd had no complaints. He supposed the time would come when he'd have to give serious consideration to settling down and perhaps producing an heir. It would be nice to pass the reins over to a son, to have him carry on the business he'd started from scratch seven years ago, but he couldn't see any need to hurry. Anyway, there was no one who interested him enough at the moment. He had to admit to himself though that his lifestyle of late was starting to bore him ever so slightly, becoming stale. He'd needed a boost and that was why he'd been so looking forward to playing golf today. He hadn't played for quite a while and the prospect of doing something completely different had filled him with a kind of excited anticipation.

Dolefully looking down at the pile of applications before him, he berated himself on his more than unethical way of choosing the new staff member, but damn it all, he really wanted . . . no needed . . . to play golf. The weather was perfect, but he could see his golf game slowly receding into the background as his good sense and sense of fair play finally reasserted themselves.

Breathing in deeply, disappointed beyond measure, he buzzed his secretary once more asking her if she'd mind going to the canteen and getting him a cup of coffee and an extra-large slice of that rich chocolate cake he couldn't stay away from. Meanwhile, he sorted through the pile of hopeful applicants whose photographs stared glassily up at him from within their open folders. His sour mood, since being called in to the office this morning, showed every indication of flourishing into a full blown attack of gigantic proportions.

"Oh, well, maybe next time," he told the empty room. It was too late now. He was stuck here in his office behind a desk while the rest of the world was off doing whatever their little hearts desired.

Melodramatic, he thought, *hell, yes, but he was entitled to a little melodrama, surely even a stately sulk or two,* he told himself resignedly. He squared his broad shoulders knowing he needed to settle down to the task at hand, that of choosing a research assistant who was also able to double as a game keeper out in the yard, or vice versa. The job description had clearly stated that the position would require the successful applicant to spend a good portion of their time working out of doors.

He categorised the applicants into piles thus thinning out their ranks substantially noting that Ms. Tarmin Elizabeth Blain; age 25; single; had made it through to the short list with effortless ease.

"Ah, Ms. Blain, we meet again," he told the glossy image once again reading through her impressive portfolio. She was certainly qualified for the position, overly so if he was any judge.

She intrigued him. She certainly couldn't be blamed for trying to land the job by using her looks and he wondered briefly why someone would purposely go out of their way to play down their feminine attributes to the extent that they looked positively drab and uninteresting. Certainly all of the women he knew literally plastered their faces with make-up and experimented with all of the latest hairstyles in an attempt to make themselves look more alluring to members of the opposite sex. He had the feeling Ms. Blain would scrub up rather well if she put her mind to it. Her bone structure was classical, high cheek bones that accentuated her face, a pert nose and from what he could determine, a nice mouth, if only she'd smile.

For some reason that he couldn't fathom this woman had gone to extraordinary lengths to make herself appear . . . what was the word he was looking for . . . dowdy. She'd almost succeeded, but not quite for there was no way she could hide her classical beauty and flawless complexion. She could throw people off the scent, and indeed probably had, but her face was a masterpiece with or without the covering of make-up. She may have chosen to work with an empty canvas, but he was a connoisseur of the female form and recognised rare beauty when he saw it even when the owner of that face had obviously gone to such an extraordinary length as to present herself in such an ordinary, unappealing package.

He wondered what it would take to bring this woman to full vibrant, throbbing life then immediately berated himself for his line of thinking. He certainly didn't want the job. He'd instigated an iron clad rule for himself way back in the early days when he'd first started his business. A rule to which he'd religiously adhered regardless of the circumstances in which he found himself. He'd promised himself that he would never, ever, mix business with pleasure. He wouldn't date one of his employees. Breaking off a relationship could get awfully sticky and complicated if the two people involved worked together. He was perfectly happy with Colleen, well moderately happy anyway, okay, not at all, he was thinking of moving on. He'd met a girl the other night while he'd been at a party. She'd been more than receptive to the idea of their spending some time together

Colleen knew the score, knew he didn't want to settle down. Hopefully, she wouldn't create a fuss when he finally told her their time together had come to an end. She'd been a delightful companion, but lately she'd been talking about commitment and that was something he shied away from preferring to be the master of his own destiny. He planned to tell her after the theatre next week. He'd found from past experience that it was better to end a relationship on a high note.

Tarmin looked about her with undisguised interest. She had arrived. She intended to find out as much information as she could about the city she'd now be calling home. Rockhampton, she already knew had a population of around seventy-six thousand. She's done a Google search on the internet before leaving Seattle and had read some of the information during the long plane flight across the Pacific before landing in Brisbane which she already knew to be the capital of Queensland. From there, she'd taken a domestic flight north to Rocky. She smiled at the abbreviation she'd used when thinking of the Central Queensland city. Most people seemed to use the shortened name, she noticed. Rockhampton was so named because of the many rock formations that were in the Fitzroy River. At least, that's what she'd been told. She guessed she'd find out for herself soon enough.

The city was about forty kilometres inland from the coast and an equal distance from the mouth of the Fitzroy River. Tarmin was surprised to read that this river was the largest in Queensland. Another four or five rivers fed into it apparently. *Ah well*, she thought, *there'll be plenty of time to find out information like that when I arrive.* There was an area on the coast known as the Capricorn Coast and a town called Yeppoon was its major centre. She'd have to make it her business to have a look around before starting work. It wouldn't do if the tourists who came to the park knew more about the place than she did. It wouldn't bode well with her new boss, she was sure, if she was the one asking all of the questions. She'd come to this position very highly recommended by her former employers who hadn't really wanted to lose her, but when her boss had realised how adamant she was to leave he'd reluctantly given in and let her go.

She didn't think her application had been successful, but then out of the blue she'd received an email informing her that the job was hers if she was still interested. The only catch was that she'd have to start immediately as time was of the essence with her new employer.

From that moment on everything had moved at a whirlwind pace as there was so much she had to do. This fast pace suited Tarmin as it gave her less time to think about the people, or person, her heart threw in that she was leaving behind. She made a mental note of the places she intended to visit in the not too distant future. The gem fields at Rubyvale looked interesting as did some of the outback towns that dotted the map she'd looked at and she'd love to visit the islands that were off the Capricorn Coast. Great Keppel Island in particular looked to be interesting. There certainly seemed to be a lot of tourist destinations in and around the city. Rockhampton was known as the beef capital of Central Queensland and she'd been interested to know that Rocky had a sister city, Ibusuki, in Japan. *All roads lead to Rockhampton,* she thought smilingly. Hers certainly had. She just hoped she'd made the right decision in coming here as she'd left a promising career at the Seattle zoo. Running away seemed to be becoming a habit since her break-up with Kel, but she couldn't bear the pain that loving him brought her. She'd run across a continent, uprooting herself from Washington D.C. to move to Seattle. Now she'd moved again, clear across the world to Australia. There was nowhere left to run.

———

Tarmin watched the truck driver skillfully manoeuvre the large van down the narrow gravel driveway. Thank goodness the last of her belongings had finally arrived and were now sitting safely in the spare room of the cottage she'd be calling home for the time being. She could go through the contents of the boxes at her leisure when time permitted which wouldn't be now she conceded abruptly to herself. She barely had enough time to shower and change her grubby clothes before going off for her job interview with her new employer. The interview was a mere formality as the position was hers.

Selecting her outfit carefully, she ran her hand slowly along a row of tailored suits. Almost of its own accord her hand stopped on a particular outfit that she knew looked good on her.

Half an hour later saw her showered, dressed and ready to leave. She gave her reflection a per-functionary nod as she passed the long oval mirror that was for now propped up against the wall in her small bedroom. She found she was satisfied with the overall result having chosen a suit of lime green, a colour which she knew accentuated her creamy skin and brought out the chestnut highlights of her hair.

She was about to make her way to her car when her attention was claimed by a noise that sounded like an animal howling in pain. This was followed by someone cursing loudly making it obviously clear that the owner of the voice was unaware he was being overheard.

"What wonderful neighbours I seem to have," Tarmin mused to herself as she continued on her way to the garage. She was mindful to step around the deep puddles of water laying on the ground. They'd been left there by the storm that had passed over the area earlier that morning.

Opening the wooden garage doors proved to be a problem. Tarmin made a mental note to have someone look at them as soon as possible. The darn things refused to budge. *Probably the rain and the colder than usual weather*, she thought irritably to herself. She gave the doors a kick for good measure before trying once more to pry them open.

"I've never known anything to work once you've kicked it," an amused voice told her from somewhere behind her causing her to jump back in fright.

Turning sharply to look in the direction of the voice she found her gaze focusing on a pair of the bluest eyes she had ever seen. *Like deep blue pools,* Tarmin thought to herself before she pulled herself up short. She didn't want to notice his eyes or anything else about him. Certainly not the fact that he was extremely tall, well over six feet and well-tanned. He probably spent all of his time out of doors. She was also forced to reluctantly admit to herself that he was extremely fit. He had dark blond hair, worn fashionably at collar length although terribly windswept at the moment. Morning stubble still adorned his face and neck, *but all in all as exteriors go,* Tarmin thought, *he was quite a sight.* She could detect deep grooves in his cheeks through the stubble and thought his dimples rounded off his good looks. *It's a good thing I'm not in the least bit interested,* she told herself forthrightly. After all forewarned is forearmed or so they say.

"It's stuck," she informed him irritably cursing herself for not being able to come up with something more intelligent than that, but this man had taken her by complete surprise appearing virtually out of thin air. That he was the owner of the voice she'd heard earlier was obvious even if his tone was kinder now that he was talking to her and not the dog he'd been cursing a few minutes ago.

"There's a knack to opening it," he told her indicating the door with a slight jerk of his head.

"What?" Tarmin asked stupidly still staring. She'd completely forgotten about the doors.

"The doors, if you lift and pull them at the same time it's a piece of cake," he repeated as if he was talking to a child.

"Lift and pull. Right I'll remember that," Tarmin told him moving out of his way as he proceeded to demonstrate the technique involved.

"See, once you know how, it's easy," he said turning to smile at her.

"Yes. Well thank you. I'd better be going. I've got a job interview. It won't look good if I'm late," now why had she told him that? She had to slip past him to gain access to the garage and her car. She found herself to be momentarily aware of his masculinity even though his appearance at the moment was less than complementary. His clothes were covered with a fine film of dust, probably from his run in with his dog, or whatever he'd been chasing earlier on. Added to that one side of his face was smeared with mud; Tarmin could tell that beneath all of that dirt there lurked a very good looking man and, what was worse, she guessed he knew it. His kind was used to woman throwing themselves at them without their having to lift a finger. Well here was one girl who was going to stay completely immune to his and any other male charms from now on. She wasn't in any particular hurry to have her heart trounced again. She was still trying to come to terms with the last beating it had taken. *Hey, enough of that,* she told herself sternly pushing the unhappy episode from her mind. Now was not the time to be thinking of Kelvin.

"Good luck," he told her pleasantly before turning on his heel to backtrack through the small hole in the fence. This was obviously the way he'd gained access to her property. She'd have to speak to the owner about fixing the hole. She didn't want him using her property as an access route or, for that matter, thinking he was welcome to pop through the fence whenever the mood took him. She wanted her privacy and would fight to preserve it.

It was only as she drove away that she realised they hadn't introduced themselves. She conceded it was probably just as well for she didn't want to strike up a friendship with him or anybody else. She was more than happy to remain anonymous, to be known only as that unfriendly redhead from next door.

Sprinting back to the house, Zac smiled unashamedly to himself as he thought of the chance meeting he'd just had with Tarmin Blain. He'd wanted to satisfy his curiosity about her and to some small extent that had been accomplished this morning.

It was a stroke of pure luck that he'd been chasing Rastus. He'd been trying to make his escape through the hole in the fence. He was amoured with the poodle down the road and tried at every opportunity to visit her. Her owners were irritated beyond belief for the poodle was a pure bred and Rastus was . . . well, poor old Rastus didn't have a pedigree to speak of. He was the original mongrel with a bit of everything thrown in, but he knew what he liked and at the moment he liked the poodle down the street.

Anyway, he'd been chasing Rastus when he'd happened to overhear her trying to open the garage doors. The recent bad weather had swollen them. It happened every time it rained, but the cottage had been empty up until now and the need to fix them hadn't been the highest point on his agenda. Thinking there's no time like the present; he changed direction and headed for his own garage. It also doubled as a small workshop. It was fitted out with an assortment of tools and labour saving devices of every description and soon he had everything he needed.

He smugly congratulated himself on being correct in his initial assumption about her being beautiful, stunningly so actually. Unlike her photograph, today she was wearing make-up, although only the merest bit. He found himself thinking that she didn't really need any enhancements to add to her overall perfection. Her long hair had been allowed to fall freely, waving naturally around her slim shoulders with just two small gold clasps behind her ears to keep it firmly in place, framing her gorgeous face with its chestnut brilliance. It looked thick and lustrous and full of shining vitality. Its colour reminded him of maple leaves once they'd fallen to the ground in the autumn. He'd been able to see the colour of her eyes and had been stunned by their unusual colour which wasn't a dark blue as he had at first thought, but a rich luscious violet. They were beautiful. He wondered briefly about the glasses, for she hadn't been wearing them and he thought that possibly she might wear contacts. *A much better alternative*, he thought. It was sacrilege to hide those beautiful eyes behind a pair of unflattering spectacles.

She had a pleasant voice laced with a slight American accent and it had amused him to hear her trying to give him the brush off, very politely mind you, but a brush off just the same. He wondered what her reaction would be when she found out that he was her boss; that she was working for him, in fact that she'd be working with him when he returned to work.

It had been ages since he'd even looked at the tools he kept. The cobwebs he'd had to demolish to get at them bore testimony to that fact, but he just didn't get the time. There weren't enough hours in his day at the present time and to prove his point his phone started to ring and he sprinted energetically up the steps hoping he wasn't going to be called back into the office.

He had at long last been able to take some much needed time off needing to recharge his worn out batteries. Now he was just about ready to take on the world again and all of the challenges that would be presented to him as Chairman of the Board of a very diverse, very busy, fast moving, still growing business, one that he'd started from scratch seven years ago. He'd seen a window of opportunity and had taken a huge gamble, financed by the generosity of his parent's life savings and their unswerving faith in their son's ability to succeed and luckily for him, and them, his gamble had handsomely paid off. He was well on his way towards gathering a small fortune for himself. His only regret was that they hadn't lived to see the empire he was building for himself.

This latest venture would firmly establish him with-in the tourism industry, an area that held his interest, but one that, as yet, he'd left virtually untapped.

Tarmin was ushered into a small room that would act as her office when she wasn't busy answering questions about Australia or conducting tours around the park.

"This is your very own hidey hole. Somewhere to escape too when you need a few minutes to yourself," her escort told her smilingly. Laura Green was a portly lady to whom Tarmin had taken immediately.

"By the sound of things that won't be very often," she
responded with enthusiasm. She much preferred the outdoors
anyway. Tarmin thought she could detect an American accent
and asked if her assumption was correct.

"Yes," was the pleasant reply, "my husband Bill works here
also. It sounds like you've picked up a bit of an accent yourself
after your years of living in the States. You'll meet Bill later.
He's around here somewhere. There'll be a small amount of
paperwork each day and the odd conference now and then, but
by and large the biggest part of your day will be outside."

Tarmin went on to tell her that she had lived in America
for fifteen years and had travelled extensively with her family
until she'd landed a job working in a wildlife park where she'd
worked for a few years in a similar environment to this one. The
company had needed her expertise about Australian wildlife
and the environment in which the wildlife lived. Her input had
been invaluable.

"Yes, I know. It's all in your C.V. Your work record is very
impressive." She didn't add that the position had been given to
another candidate who, at the last minute, had refused the job
for a more lucrative offer overseas where the opportunity for
advancement was far better. They'd been desperate for the girl
was to have started immediately. Zac, unperturbed, had pulled
Tarmin's file out of his desk drawer telling his aunt to offer her
the position. They had then waited three weeks for her to arrive
into the country. She'd been offered the use of the small cottage
adjoining Zac's place until such time as she could establish
herself in another home which might be more to her liking.
Tarmin had loved the place and had asked if her stay could be
on a more permanent basis.

Laura asked casually, making conversation, "How in the world did your boss manage to convince the powers-that-be that something like this would work? I didn't think it would be allowed, isn't everything in Washington government run?"

"Heavens no," Tarmin told her, thinking back to her time spent in Washington D.C. before she had moved to Seattle. She then launched into a lively spiel about some of the tourist destinations that Washington had to offer to the tourist, "Take the Folger Shakespeare Library and the Museum of African Art. They're both private institutions. Both worthy of visiting by the way if you're planning a trip back home in the near future." their conversation was cut short when a female head was poked unceremoniously around the door.

"You're wanted on the phone, Mrs. Green," the head said before disappearing again.

"Okay, Millie, be right with you. Tarmin, come with me please. You've made me feel quite homesick. I want to hear some more." Tarmin's only option was to follow her retreating figure down the hallway to a large office where a heavily be-ringed hand indicated for her to sit down on one of the white cane chairs that had been strategically placed near a large bay window. She whispered, "I won't be long." before she gave her full attention to her caller.

Tarmin took the time to look around her with interest. Laura, Mrs. Green had insisted on first names, was talking excitedly to someone, presumably her husband judging by the way the tone of her voice had shifted from a woman in authority to a low seductive whisper.

The office was flamboyantly decorated. Laura had boldly splashed out using bright vivid colours to their best advantage.

The room was nearly as colourful as Tarmin expected its owner to be, full of vibrant life, not at all barren and cold as most offices seemed to be these days. Tarmin loved it.

The large mural on the far wall caught her eye. Colours were splashed haphazardly across the canvas in total abandonment with red's, blue's, bright yellow's and vibrant green's all merging into each other to form a painting that totally captured the imagination of the onlooker. She looked for a signature, but couldn't see one which led her to wonder if Laura had been the artist. Cheerful was the word that sprang to mind as Tarmin soaked up the room's welcoming atmosphere. On the other side of the bay window, which looked out into the heart of the park, there was a similar chair to the one she occupied. Separating them was a glass topped occasional table and diagonally across the room there was a large three seater cane sofa. All had been decorated with brightly covered throw cushions which added delightfully to the overall effect of the room. She'd defy anyone to be sad in this room.

"It's beautiful, isn't it?" Laura said, coming to stand next to Tarmin and both women stood looking out at the beauty of the surrounding parklands.

"Yes," she said simply knowing instinctively that no further answer was needed.

Her mind flashed back momentarily to another country and another park, both of which were quite beautiful also. The park where she had worked would now be covered with a fine spattering of snow from the first falls of the season. Soon, she knew, there would be a winter wonderland of snow and icicles hiding the green grass until the winter thaw.

Feeling a momentary pang of longing for the country she'd so recently left Tarmin heaved a small sigh and continued to daydream as memories came flooding back into her mind, some of which still caused her a considerable amount of pain.

———

Later that night, while sitting on the floor knee deep in boxes and packing paper and wondering where on earth she was going to put everything Tarmin let her mind return to her thoughts of that afternoon and her eyes misted over with tears as they always did when she thought of Kelvin and the love they'd shared. She'd made the right decision in coming back to Australia. Now instead of only a continent being between them there was also an immense ocean helping to keep them apart.

To make matters worse, when she'd arrived home this afternoon there was a letter from her sister informing her that she was going to be an aunty again. Kelvin and Carrie were expecting their second child. There'd also been a gentle dig as to when she was going to return the favour.

Probably never, Tarmin thought to herself. It wasn't that the thought of having children was repulsive to her, no, quite the opposite, in fact there'd been a time when having a family to look after was all she'd ever wanted out of life, but it seemed to her that life had other plans for Tarmin Blain.

She'd been going out with Kelvin Simpson for nearly two years. She'd truly believed their love for each other had been the strong and durable kind. She knew with an all knowing certainty that her feelings had been iron clad, still were she told herself sadly. It was true that there hadn't been any talk of marriage between them, but she'd been sure that it was just a matter of time before they'd take that all important next step.

Then out of the blue her sister, Carrie, had turned up at her apartment asking if she could stay because she wanted to escape from a disastrous relationship and wham that was it; before all three of them knew what was happening Kelvin and Carrie had fallen hopelessly in love.

At first, Tarmin tried pretending nothing out of the ordinary was happening, but it was becoming more evident with every passing day that a strong attraction had been formed between the two of them. She'd done the only thing possible telling Kelvin that she didn't love him leaving him free to marry Carrie which he did two months later. Now almost three years down the track they were still crazily in love and about to present both families with another grandchild.

Tarmin's mother was the only one she'd been able to confide in; the only one who realised how much her eldest daughter was hurting, how much she'd loved Kelvin. Tarmin found it hard to act like a friend and sister-in-law and had literally jumped at the position in Seattle when it had been offered to her making the move from Washington D.C. to the west coast. It was just too painful to watch the two of them together. Now twelve months later she'd come back to Australia still running away from her past and the hurt which was still being inflicted onto her wounded heart.

She'd dated occasionally over the last three years, but her heart had remained untouched. She despaired of ever finding another man to whom she could freely give her love.

Her melancholy thoughts were interrupted by the ringing of the telephone and Tarmin was almost glad of the intrusion for it brought her mind back to the present.

She was surprised to hear Laura's voice on the other end of the line. "Tarmin, how are you? Settling in alright?"

When Tarmin affirmed that she was Laura went on, "I've just remembered that I forgot to tell you about the staff get together we're having at my place next weekend. It will be an excellent opportunity for you to meet and greet your fellow workers in an informal atmosphere before you actually start work. They're a good bunch. I'm sure you'll get along famously with them all."

Tarmin listened, very much amused and wondered when Laura was going to stop talking and come up for air. When she was finally given the opportunity to speak she affirmed that she'd be able to come. All she had planned for the weekend was a visit to the gym, but that could be postponed until Sunday.

"By the way," Laura wanted to know, asking casually, "have you met any of your new neighbours yet?"

"Not really, no," Tarmin didn't count her early morning visitor because they hadn't really introduced themselves and she didn't think she'd be seeing him again anyway. *At least not any time soon*, she thought, unless his dog planned another trip through the hedge.

"You don't sound very sure," Laura teased.

"Well, no, it's not that. I was talking to someone this morning. I guess he was a neighbour. He helped me to open my garage doors." Tarmin went on to tell Laura about her visitor adding, "We didn't introduce ourselves, so technically I haven't met any of my neighbours."

"What was he like, worth remembering?" Laura wanted to know. Her tone was slightly bantering.

"I guess so if you like his sort of looks," Tarmin answered slowly as her mind flashed back to recreate a perfect image of the man from this morning.

"And did you?" Laura probed fishing for an answer.

"I didn't really take that much notice," Tarmin lied. An instant image manifested itself in her mind of a man with vivid blue eyes, blond hair, gorgeously cute dimples, tanned, well-built and extremely tall. *No, she hadn't noticed him very much at all.*

"Oh well," Laura told her flippantly, "If you meet him again take a closer look. He might be a nice young man."

"A nice young man," Tarmin interjected not really wanting this particular conversation to continue on its present course. She just wasn't interested. She was relieved when Laura finally changed the subject and started talking about other things.

———

Over the next few days Tarmin was kept busy whipping her little cottage into livable order. She'd been very grateful to Laura for suggesting she stay here. There was a rustic charm about the place which appealed to her sense of rightness. She especially loved the assortment of wildlife which seemed to inhabit the shrubbery and trees that grew wild in the back yard. She'd started leaving tiny morsels of food and an assortment of grains in accessible locations hoping to entice some of the animals and birds out into the open.

Today she'd decided to eat her lunch outside on the steps. Looking towards the sky she noticed it was cloud free and a beautiful clear blue. She'd heard on the radio that they might have some more rain, but if that was the case it was a long way off.

Tarmin was thrilled when within a few minutes of her sitting down a small flock of galahs swooped down to land on the make shift perches she'd constructed and had started to eat the honeyed grain she'd spread out on some old metal plates only this morning. When she had some more time she planned to put in a bird bath and attach some hanging feeders from the branches of the surrounding trees. She enjoyed the sounds of their chirping and was content to sit back and quietly watch them while they happily devoured the food she'd left out for them. Perhaps she'd be able to put up some breeding boxes. She could monitor their progress quite easily without disturbing them.

Breathing deeply, she filled her nostrils with the sweet air loving the pungent aroma of the wild flowers as their scent wafted up from the garden bed located directly beneath her. The water puddles of a few days ago were fast drying up and were now no more than small muddy bogs waiting for the sun to completely dry them out.

Her attention was claimed by some movement coming from the other side of the hedge that separated the two properties from each other. She was surprised and also a little bit alarmed to see a giant of a dog inching its way slowly on its belly through the small opening in the hedge. Once inside her yard it sprang to its feet and shook itself off sending dirt and twigs flying off in every direction. It then turned and headed happily down the driveway quite oblivious to the fact that its escape had been witnessed.

Oh well, thought Tarmin. *It's not my problem. Anyway, it could be dangerous; it could have bitten me if I'd tried to stop it.* She was certain that the dog must have chosen this avenue of escape on a regular basis for it had seemed to know exactly in which direction it had wanted to go. She sighed wearily thinking she'd have to see the man next door and ask him to do something about his dog using her premises as an escape route.

"Rastus, you dumb mutt, where are you?" a man's clear voice broke the tranquility which was surrounding her. The birds, also startled by the sudden noise, rose together in a flurry of wings flying off to another part of the surrounding bush land where they knew they'd be safe.

Tarmin thought she should call out to him letting him know that his dog had escaped down her driveway. She was just a little bit miffed that his loud voice had scared the birds away and had also intruded on the serenity she'd been enjoying. She decided to stay quiet, thinking that perhaps he'd go away and look elsewhere for his straying dog.

She didn't want to get involved with her neighbour; didn't want to start casual conversations about his dog or anything else for that matter that might, or might not lead to other things. She didn't want to get involved with him on any level, knowing that choosing that particular path one could get hurt and she was still smarting from her last bout of unrequited love. She didn't want, or need to be reminded that her heart wasn't ready to be trounced yet again by any man. She was in no particular hurry to repeat the experience. Once had been more than enough.

Sadly, the decision was taken out of her hands when a few minutes later the man who had just been occupying her thoughts came striding around the corner of her cottage, his face grim. He stopped short when he saw her sitting on the small sundeck and threw her an apologetic half smile before he proceeded to explain what he was doing on her side of the hedge yet again.

Involuntarily, Tarmin's eyes were drawn to his face. She didn't want to notice him, especially those vivid blue eyes and finely arched brows, drawn together now as he explained to her about his wayward, lovesick dog.

Almost against her will, her senses were reacting to him and she let her eyes travel down the length of him and back again. She suppressed a slight smile as she read the slogan, 'Save the Whales,' which was emblazoned on the front of his t-shirt in large, bright, red letters. His jeans fitted him snugly around his hips and thighs before tapering down his long legs to where his bare feet were exposed on the gravel path.

"Your dog went that-a-way," Tarmin motioned with a quick jerk of her head towards the front gate which she knew was wide open, "You've just missed him by a couple of minutes. If you hurry you'll catch him before he gets too far." Upon saying this she rose from the steps where she'd been sitting and walked inside leaving him standing staring after her with a quizzical expression plastered onto his face.

Zac stood watching her retreating figure for a few seconds more, appreciating the casual swing of her shapely hips as she swaggered away, her legs weren't too bad either he conceded before the closed door obliterated his view. She was wearing a pair of very short shorts that had showed her long limbs off to perfection. Swallowing slowly he dragged his mind back to his initial reason for being here and sprinted down the driveway after his pest of a dog. He'd deal with Ms. Blain's unfriendly attitude at a later date, but for now Rastus had to be his first priority.

Tarmin wouldn't allow herself to look back once she was inside, although she'd wanted too. She resolutely walked through to the other side of the cottage into the kitchen where she knew she wouldn't be able to see him and sat down at the table.

She knew she'd been rude in the way she'd practically shunned him, but now perhaps he'd get the message about leaving her alone. She didn't want to cultivate a friendship that would see them popping over to each other's place to share coffee, or to pass the time of day, or anything else. She just wanted to be left alone to live her life in the way that suited her.

"He's got a cute tush," Tarmin told the empty room and was immediately horrified at the way her erratic thoughts were travelling. "Hold it right there, girlie!" she berated herself sternly. *Where in the world had that thought come from. Get off this wavelength*, she thought soberly, *or before you know it you'll be mooning over some man you don't even know,* "And don't want to know!" she reinforced loudly to the empty room. Anyway, she told herself exaltedly, after the brush off you just gave him, he'll think twice about engaging you in any sort of conversation from now on.

———

Feeling full of nervous energy Tarmin decided on the spur of the moment to visit the gym. It would be her first visit since joining and she knew she was well overdue for a vigorous workout. Grabbing a towel and filling her water bottle she headed out the back door. She popped a piece of gum into her mouth, a habit she'd picked up while living in America. She decided she was now ready to face the world

Her spontaneous attitude lasted only a few minutes longer for when she reached the garage doors she could see that they were welded shut again from the rain.

Tarmin stood, hands on hips, and surveyed the doors telling them pertly, "You think you've won, don't you? Well I'm here to tell you that you're very greatly mistaken. I plan to get you open."

Rubbing her hands together with a determination she was far from feeling she advanced towards her intended prey. She gave the doors a good hard shake and was rewarded when she felt them give a little beneath her grasp.

"Round one to me," Tarmin informed the inanimate object in front of her, "Now what was it next door said to do?" She stood thinking about what she'd been told to do. "Lift and pull, that's it," she said triumphantly as she tried to do just that.

This proved to be easier said than done and after only a few minutes of trying to prise open the doors Tarmin stood back panting slightly regarding the doors absentmindedly still chewing vigorously on her gum. She had just blown a rather large bubble when a now familiar voice greeted her.

"You know in that get up and doing that, you look about twelve years old." Before she could come up with a suitable answer, he continued, "Having trouble with your doors again?"

Tarmin felt herself blush as she turned around to face him. She pushed the gum to the side of her mouth and regarded him casually not really knowing what she could say to him. He certainly didn't seem to have any regard for the fact that he was trespassing on her side of the fence. She supposed he was used to having the place to himself and probably used her driveway as a short cut, but he was going to have to stop because she didn't like it.

"The rain has warped them. I'll have to get onto the owner. Does this happen often, do you know?" Tarmin had meant the doors.

"Every year around this time," her neighbour told her blandly and Tarmin knew instinctively that he meant the storms. He was goading her deliberately, *but why is he picking on me*, she thought heatedly?

Taking a deep breath she answered through clenched teeth, "The doors . . . I meant the doors."

"Oh," he said completely drenching his masculine features with a thoughtful expression as he pretended to contemplate her words, "the doors . . . yes, it happens every time we get a lot of rain."

Tarmin was really starting to get exasperated. All doubt was now gone that he was playing with her. This was probably his way of paying her back for her rudeness to him earlier. She was determined she wasn't going to rise to the bait he was throwing out to her. He could take his silly games and get lost. *Why couldn't he stay out of her yard?*

Changing the subject and the mood of the conversation Tarmin asked, "Has your dog run away again? He didn't come through the hedge this time."

Taking his cue from her Zac told her, "No, he's at home. Chained up for good measure until I can fix the fence, but the trouble is he fancies he's in love with the poodle down the block, so for the next few days he'll have to behave or I've threatened him with a trip to the vet."

"Oh," Tarmin answered lamely. She couldn't think of a witty comeback then told herself she didn't need one. *What's wrong with me? I'm not usually tongue tired around people I like.* Her heart started hammering inside her chest as she realised the words her mind had just registered. *But I don't want to like him*, she thought frantically. I don't even know his name. This is ridiculous, things like this just don't happen.

"Hey, are you alright? I wouldn't hurt the dumb mutt, you know." He'd noticed the emotions flowing unchecked over her face and attributed her loss of colour to his remarks about Rastus. She'd looked like she was going to keel over.

Grabbing onto the excuse he'd handed her Tarmin stared up at him almost thankfully. Anything was better than having him think she was becoming attracted to him.

"I'm fine. As for your dog I don't really care what you do with it except to keep it out of my yard in future." Upon saying this she turned away from him and strode back inside, walking quickly down the hallway to the front door, stopping only long enough to fling her towel and bag onto the kitchen table. She'd go for a walk instead of going to the gym. Anything was preferable to staying in the immediate vicinity of that hateful man.

CHAPTER TWO

||||||||||||||||||||||||||||||||

The situation was totally ridiculous, Tarmin thought as she sipped a sweet, hot cup of tea a few hours later. She had literally walked the streets for hours trying to cleanse her mind of her new neighbour and the thoughts that he'd started to evoke within her.

I can't keep running away every time I set eyes on him. *He probably thinks I'm a total idiot already*, she thought. Big tears rolled unchecked down her pale cheeks. It wasn't fair. She didn't want to get involved with anyone. Her thoughts reverted to earlier times to the man she still loved with all of her heart. His tall bronzed image swam before her eyes. Warm, loving, brown eyes caressed her responsive body, loving her, needing her. Tender hands roved over her soft curves reminding her of her womanly attributes. Tarmin moaned knowing she had to intrude on her erratic thoughts. Kelvin was now out of reach and unattainable. He was married to her sister. These erotic thoughts of him had to stop.

Setting her cup down on the floor beside the divan she gave in to her melancholy mood and had a good cry. "He can only be a problem if I let him bother me," Tarmin told herself staunchly a bit later as she washed away all traces of her tears.

Next morning she was astonished by the sight that greeted her. Not only were her obstinate garage doors open, but she could see that they had been replaced.

After her walk yesterday she'd used the front door of the cottage to get inside and hadn't ventured out the back for fear of running into her neighbour.

Tarmin looked around her in astonishment. Who could have done this work? But more to the point, when was it done?

Surely her neighbour hadn't . . . but it was the only logical explanation she was able to come up with, but why!

Why couldn't he leave her alone and stay out of her life. His continued presence on her side of the fence was the only dark cloud on her horizon. She'd just started a new job in a new city, not to mention another country and she didn't want to be tormented by someone who couldn't keep to his own side of the boundary line. She didn't want any involvement with anyone, especially with someone who practically lived on her doorstep.

"Admiring my handiwork?"

Spinning around Tarmin was caught off guard again by this man who seemed to feel just as much at home here in her yard as he did in his own judging by the amount of time he spent over here.

"You didn't have to do this," she told him ungraciously, "I was going to contact the owner today."

"I usually do all of the renovations if it's needed," he told her. Well it was true. He did fix most of the things around the place sooner or later; in this instance it had been later.

"What do I owe you for this?" she flung caustically at him, astounded by her own harsh words and actions.

"Nothing, let's just say I was being neighbourly," Zac answered. There was something about Tarmin Blain that intrigued him. He couldn't put his finger on the problem, but he was sure before too long he'd work out why she fascinated him so much.

"Look, I appreciate what you've done, but I'd also appreciate being left alone and I'd appreciate it if you could keep your dog on your side of the fence." Tarmin felt mean but she felt it was better to get things out in the open between them while he was here. Then perhaps he'd stay away.

Zac looked down at her for a long minute and his reaction to her outburst was totally unexpected and very swift. One minute he'd turned and had started to walk away, but before Tarmin knew what was happening he rotated on his heel and gathered her unresistingly up into his arms and began to kiss her soundly on the lips.

Gasping in delayed shock Tarmin tried to push herself away from him, but this action only served to make her mouth, and its sweetness, more accessible to him. Her mind fought him off for a few seconds longer then her natural instincts took over. Forgetting her resolution of a few seconds ago about not wanting to become involved with this man she started to return his kiss with a vengeance that would have surprised her had she been capable of rational thought at that particular moment. How long they stood locked together she couldn't say, but she knew it was all too soon when they finally parted.

"There, Ms. Blain, consider the debt paid in full," Zac told her. His eyes glittered like bright blue sapphires as he looked down at her. They held a wry amusement at the abandoned way in which she'd responded to his kiss.

Tarmin lifted unsteady fingers to her trembling lips; they were still tingling from the surprise contact between them. What a hypocrite he probably thought her. Adamantly telling him on the one hand she didn't want to know him then joining in so wholeheartedly when he kissed her. It didn't occur to her to ask him how he knew her name. Her mind hadn't registered that he'd addressed her at all. She was still trying to come to terms with the mammoth implications that kiss presented her with.

Tarmin neither heard nor saw her neighbour for the next few days. Her bemused mind didn't know whether to be happy or sad about the circumstances in which she found herself. Also, there was no sign of the dog so she presumed he was still unhappily tied up until he was over his bout of lovesickness.

Her garage doors now opened and shut without the slightest bit of trouble, *pity*, she thought sheepishly. She found she was actually trying to think up excuses to go over there. Damn! What was wrong with her, had she lost her marbles. Marching herself resolutely inside, Tarmin bolted the door then smiled wryly to herself as she thought of the implications of her rash action. A bolted door wouldn't save her, she told herself sadly while her traitorous mind began to conjure up a certain male of the species whose eyes had the ability to taunt her from their blue depths.

The shrill ringing of the telephone saved her from any more soul searching and she answered it gladly, happy to be talking to someone. "Hi there, all set for this afternoon?" a cheery voice wanted to know.

Tarmin smiled into the receiver. "Yes," she told Laura. This was just what her bruised ego needed. An afternoon out in the company of other people would take her mind off certain other problems. "I've decided not to drive though. Getting lost last week has dampened my enthusiasm for driving in this place so I'll get a taxi." Tarmin still felt embarrassed about her little side trip to the coast, well, it was supposed to be to the coast, but she'd missed the turn and had actually been heading north up the highway towards Mackay.

"Not to worry. I've arranged a ride for you. That's one of the reasons I rang. My nephew lives close by and as he is driving over I asked him if he'd mind dropping by to pick you up," Laura said. Her voice sounded slightly comical almost like she was stifling a laugh.

"Thank you, that would be very nice," Tarmin told her host pleasantly, but she would have preferred to find her own way. She supposed she could stand her boss' nephew for the short amount of time it would take for them to reach their destination.

"Fine all settled. I've told him to pick you up at two thirty." Upon saying this Laura hung up leaving Tarmin gazing down at the receiver in her hand. She fervently hoped that her boss wasn't delving into any matchmaking. To have someone trying to find her someone to go out with was the last thing she needed in her life at the present time.

Tarmin was ready well before two-thirty that afternoon. Although dressed casually she looked attractive in the outfit she'd chosen. She didn't believe in being a slave to fashion and chose her wardrobe according to her personal taste which she knew could sometimes be a bit bazaar. Today she'd chosen conservatively and was wearing black linen slacks with a plain ultramarine blue blouse which helped to highlight the golden highlights in her chestnut hair.

Her door chimes sounded just before two-thirty and Tarmin promptly opened the door to stare up into the face of her neighbour. She was appalled and she knew her discomfort must be registering on her pale features.

"You!" she said, without decorum, "What do you want?" Her mind involuntarily returned to their last encounter and the kiss they had shared. She could feel her face starting to flame as unwanted memories intruded into her thoughts bringing with them an unwelcome longing which she tried to push unsuccessfully aside. He was the last person she'd expected to see. Thank goodness her ride should be here soon and she could make her escape. Looking past him down the driveway she hoped Laura's nephew wouldn't be too much longer.

Zac turned around wanting to know what she was looking at, but he could see nothing; then it dawned on him that she was waiting to be picked up, but she didn't know by whom.

"This time I think introductions are in order, don't you? My name is Zac Coghlan. Laura Green is my aunt and I've been asked to escort you to the party. Are you ready to go?"

"You're Zac Coghlan!" Tarmin could feel every ounce of colour draining away from her face. No! Her mind screamed as she looked at him. This can't be possible

"At your service." He sent her a small grin which was accompanied by a half bow. This would have softened the heart of any other girl, but Tarmin merely pursed her lips and wondered if there was any way in which she could extricate herself from this afternoon's festivity without arousing any suspicions.

"I wasn't going to go," she told him. There was no way she was going to spend an afternoon in this man's company.

Looking at her shrewdly Zac thought he recognised the source of her discomfort. "Look, about the other day, I know I was out of line when I kissed you. I guess I owe you an apology. You made me mad. I was only trying to be neighbourly you know."

"You guess you owe me an apology! I think I would have preferred to be welcomed in the old fashioned way," Tarmin threw at him in a tightly controlled voice.

"No, damn it, by fixing your garage doors! You're very prickly aren't you? I thought Yanks were supposed to be friendly," he told her going on the defensive.

"I am not prickly! And I'm not American, I'm Australian. I just don't like being kissed against my will."

"Oh, that explains it," he answered chuckling to himself, "Next time I'll remember to ask your permission, shall I?"

"There's not going to be a next time," Tarmin assured him through tightly clenched lips. She threw in a venomous look for good measure, but it was wasted on him for he was looking at his watch and when he looked back up at her his demeanor had changed and she could see the banter of a few seconds ago had been replaced by a more serious expression.

"Come on, or we'll be late," he told her casually, already making his way to his car which was parked in the driveway at the side of the cottage.

———

Tarmin concentrated on the scenery as it flashed past. It was certainly safer to feast her eyes on the beautiful greens and browns of the Australian landscape rather than on her companion. It also struck her as to how clean it was here. Although to be fair to her adopted country it had been beautiful too and she had loved living there; had things worked out differently between herself and Kelvin she would have been happy never to leave, but fate had had other plans.

While Tarmin was here in Australia enjoying this beautiful summer weather her family, she knew, would be gearing up for the coming winter months. Her dad would be chopping wood for the fireplace; her mum would be cooking those yummy treats she so loved to eat when she'd been home. Yet here, Down Under, people were heading to the beach in droves trying to find some relief from the harsh Australian sun.

Sighing softly to herself, Tarmin felt a tinge of homesickness for the country and the people she'd left behind. Without warning, tears pricked her eyes and she tried to rapidly blink them back before her companion could detect their unwanted presence.

"Hey, are you alright?" Zac's voice intruded upon her thoughts holding a mixture of concern and anxiety. The last thing he wanted to contend with was a crying female, even one as beautiful as Ms. Tarmin Elizabeth Blain.

"Yes, I'm fine. I was just comparing climates," she told him by way of an explanation.

"Yes, I can see how that would upset you," he answered flippantly, sending her a strange look.

"Don't make fun of me. Thinking of home made me think of my family. I miss them."

"I thought you said you weren't American?" he asked idly as he negotiated the difficult turn that would bring them to the gates of his aunt's property.

"I'm not, but my family live in the States. My father was in the Army. He was attached to the Pentagon for a while as an Australian aide. My sister and I were typical army brats following our parents from place to place until they retired a few years ago. Dad loved it over there and decided to buy a little place on the outskirts of Washington D.C."

"Hence the slight accent?"

"I guess."

"Do you miss anyone else in particular?" he asked casually.

Tarmin thought instantly of Kelvin. For so long he'd taken up all of her memories. Her face softened as she remembered their time together, times never to be repeated, but still not completely forgotten.

Zac interpreted the look and wondered who the guy was. He was surprised that he really wanted to know.

"No, not anymore," Tarmin responded although her voice softened and sounded husky even to her own ears.

"Why?" he persisted needing to know why her voice had taken on that dreamy, silken quality. *If this guy meant nothing to her*, he thought, *why was she practically purring at the thought of him.*

"Are you always this nosey? Just because you're giving me a lift does it mean that I have to divulge my whole life story to you," She felt irate that she'd let her guard slip in front of this insufferable man. He was the last person on earth that she'd have wanted to talk to about Kelvin.

"Just making conversation," Zac answered put out by the fact that she wouldn't impart the information to him.

"Is it much further?" Tarmin asked, changing the subject in the hope that he'd get the message she was sending him about not delving into her private affairs. She didn't want to continue with this line of conversation, aimed as it was towards her past.

"No, we've arrived," he told her wishing he had a bit more time to talk to her by himself. He was sure that when they went inside she'd make herself scarce and stay out of his immediate vicinity. He'd considered driving around the block a couple of times but then dismissed the idea as silly.

Tarmin climbed out of the car as soon as she could safely do so. Being in such close proximity to Zac was starting to tell on her nerves. She decided she needed to put some distance between them.

"Well thank you for the lift," Tarmin told him looking at him across the roof of the car.

"Hold on. It's customary to walk in with your date, you know," he told her with an amused lilt in his voice. He couldn't help himself; he just had to see what her reaction would be to his baiting.

"Date, since when does giving someone a lift constitute a date?" Tarmin demanded hotly feeling slightly on edge. *Surely he doesn't think I'm going to spend all of my time plastered to his side*, she thought desperately wanting to escape. His close proximity was doing strange things to her body. Feelings were emerging she'd been trying to keep buried. She didn't want them spilling out for his scrutiny.

Zac was beside her now, reaching for her hand. "Don't look so worried, I promise I won't bite," but the twinkle was back in his eyes and on a stupid impulse he said, "Does this mean you want to wait to announce our engagement to the world?"

Tarmin was astounded. She didn't know how to respond to this kind of flirtatious banter, but common sense told her the best course of action was to ignore him. The last thing she wanted, or needed, was to get involved with her nosy neighbour.

"Listen carefully. I don't want to become involved in any casual relationship with you or anyone else so I'd appreciate it very much if you'd stop this nonsense immediately."

"Got it, you would rather have a long engagement." Zac didn't know why he was persisting with this line of conversation. He could see she was getting angry and if he didn't start to behave he knew she'd probably deck him right where he stood, but for the life of him he couldn't help himself. He reasoned it must have something to do with her flashing violet eyes and long chestnut curls. No other woman had ever affected him in this way before. He wanted to hold her, to kiss her, but for now he knew he would have to wait.

Pulling himself together he told her matter-of-factly, "Come on, it's too hot out here. A man's brains are in danger of being fried." Reaching out for her hand again he pulled her along after him leaving her with no choice but to follow him inside.

The party was in full swing when they were ushered inside. Zac sought out his aunt and having spied her made a beeline in her direction with Tarmin still in tow depositing her before his aunt like an unopened gift.

"Here she is, Aunt Laura, delivered safe and sound, the newest member of the team." He then turned to Tarmin to wink at her blatantly. "You can do the honours and introduce her to everyone while I get her a drink."

"Zac, hold on," Laura called her nephew, but he didn't turn around or acknowledge in any way that he'd heard.

"Isn't that just like a man to ignore you, my Dear," Laura was saying, but Tarmin was staring at his retreating head.

"Laura, why didn't you tell me that my boss was also my neighbour? After all, forewarned is forearmed, and all of that," Tarmin told her hostess pointedly.

"I assumed he'd tell you himself. It's strange that he didn't. I guess he had his reasons. He is the most unbelievable young man, don't you think?"

"Yes, unbelievable," Tarmin muttered somberly under her breath. Why hadn't he introduced himself earlier she wondered? He could have quite easily introduced himself when they'd bumped into each other at the cottage when he'd been chasing his dog. He'd had ample opportunities since then to do so as well. It would have made things a lot simpler from her point of view. She would have known where the boundaries were and could have stayed within the safety of their confines. Had she known he was someone to be respected she would have never lost her temper. She hoped it hadn't reduced her chances of working with him.

"I take it my nephew has made a less than favourable impression on you?" Laura Green asked smiling across at Zac.

"No, it's not that exactly. He just seems to turn up at the most inopportune times when I least expect him." Tarmin went on to tell Laura about the happenings of the last few days carefully omitting the part about their shared kiss.

"Those doors," Laura tutted, "I told him to fix them ages ago when we first knew you were coming."

"Is he your maintenance man as well?" Tarmin asked innocently.

"Good heavens no, but he is your landlord," Laura told an astonished Tarmin.

"But I thought you owned the cottage?" She responded thoroughly confused.

Laura smiled indulgently. "No, it belonged to Zac's mother. In the old days it was used as a guest house. We persuaded Zac to rent it to you when we realised you'd be looking for accommodation."

Any answer Tarmin might have given was forestalled as Zac came striding back with her drink which he handed to her saying, "I took a guess on what I thought you'd like . . . white wine okay?"

"Perfect, thank you. Your aunt tells me you're my landlord. Why couldn't you have told me yourself?" Tarmin's eyes bored into him, willing him to tell her the truth.

"I was going to tell you that first day. Actually that's one of the reasons I came over, but you weren't very receptive to any conversation I tried to make, then or since, so I decided to bide my time and let nature take its course." He had a way of making Tarmin feel like she was the guilty party, which she supposed she was if she took the time to rationalise the situation between them. Never-the-less, his words still rankled.

"What do you mean let nature take its course?" Tarmin's mind flew back to the passionate kiss they'd shared. Surely he didn't think there could ever be anything between them. If only her body could be persuaded into believing this. It was reacting to his nearness in an impossible way.

"I mean that once you got over your fit of temper or whatever it is that's making you so prickly towards me you might find out that I can be a nice guy. It might also surprise you to know that I don't want a relationship either, but there's no reason why we can't be friends is there?" He wondered why those few simple words spoken with such venom should rankle him so much. He didn't want a relationship so why was he being so prickly all of a sudden.

Tarmin knew those words uttered so harshly should ease her mind as to his intentions towards her. He'd just told her he wasn't interested, hadn't he? Instead they filled her with a deep loneliness that she found hard to understand. He was watching her, waiting patiently for an answer so why was she so loathe giving it to him.

"Well," he prompted.

"You're right, of course. There is absolutely no reason why we can't be friends I suppose." Tarmin agreed grudgingly, feeling as if the words were being dragged out of her.

"Does this mean the engagement is off?" she asked him innocently hoping her words would calm things down between them.

Her ploy worked for she was instantly treated to a dimpled grin which had her pulse beating erratically. His next action took her completely by surprise. Stepping closer he planted a quick kiss onto her lips before he told her, "Being friends with you is certainly going to be a challenge, but then I love a challenge."

Tarmin felt herself blush at his act of forwardness. Glancing around the room she was relieved to note that no one had noticed the intimate contact which had taken place between them.

The rest of the afternoon passed quickly. Tarmin found herself drawn to the people with whom she was going to be working. She was looking forward to Monday with a heartfelt enthusiasm. Even the thought of working with Zac wasn't enough to dampen her spirits completely.

She'd been told that Zac was strictly administration and rarely ventured out into the wilderness as he called it so the likelihood of their bumping into each other would be fairly minimal. The only time their paths would cross would be when she had to make up her reports. She was quick to notice how all of the unattached females were trying to latch themselves onto Zac's arm either by starting a conversation or on one occasion the girl in question actually pressed herself between him and the buffet table. She whispered something in his ear that had him smiling. Tarmin could imagine what it was. Her traitorous mind conjured up an image of the two of them and she found she was disturbed by what she was thinking knowing without conscious thought she wanted to be the one being held in his strong, masculine arms.

She'd done a complete summersault from pushing him away realising that her feelings for him went deeper than even she cared to admit. This could prove to be distrastrous given their conversation of a little while ago.

"Enjoying yourself?" Zac wanted to know when he joined her a few minutes later.

"Yes. I think I'm going to enjoy working for Laura. Everyone else seems to be friendly as well from what I've been able to detect." She'd let him draw his own conclusions as to the meaning of her lightly spoken comment.

"Actually you'll be working for me. Laura is my personal assistant. Does that pose a problem for you, Ms. Blain?" He asked casually enough but Tarmin sensed a deeper meaning hidden beneath his words.

"No problem," she told him simply, aware that her heart had started thumping unaccountably within her chest.

"Good." Placing a proprietary arm around her shoulders he drew her closer into the hard contours of his body. Tarmin knew she shouldn't encourage such closeness, but found she liked the feelings that started surging up throughout her body at his casual touch. She also realised the folly of becoming involved with a man with whom she was about to start a working relationship.

They stayed for a few hours longer before telling Laura they were leaving. Tarmin felt content knowing she'd made her peace with Zac.

Silence permeated throughout the car on the drive home, but it was a companionable silence and Tarmin didn't feel the need to break it. She was happy to sieve through her thoughts knowing that perhaps she had finally started to open the shutters that had encased her heart for so long thus allowing her love for Kelvin to fade ever so slightly into the background. She found Zac to be disturbingly attractive, but had valiantly fought against that attraction. She hadn't wanted to enter into another relationship where she could quite possibly be the loser.

Zac drove automatically into his own driveway, a point that Tarmin was quick to mention.

"I realise that. I thought you might like a cup of coffee." Seeing her slight hesitation he added pointedly. "You're quite safe, you know if the answer is no than I will take you right home, no problem . . . straight through the hedge," to further emphasise his point he cheekily indicated towards the fence with a flick of his hand.

Tarmin smiled despite herself, feeling foolish. Her hesitation hadn't been because she feared him. No, she was afraid she'd be in danger of giving in to him. Being with him in a crowded room was one thing, in a roomful of people she'd been able to school her emotions, but here in his home she was on her own with no one to turn to for help if her feelings got the better of her.

She realised he was waiting patiently for her to answer. Heaven only knew how long she'd been daydreaming. She'd have to think of an excuse to put him off.

"Well," he demanded in a slightly impatient voice.

"I'd love some." The words were out of her mouth before she even realised she'd uttered them. *Well so much for keeping him at a distance*, she thought wryly to herself as she followed him inside.

His house was the typical male domain showing all of the ear markings of a bachelor existence. It wasn't untidy, far from it, but there was a marked absence of any female contribution. Football trophies lined one wall plus a number of photos that had obviously been taken when he was much younger. In them, Tarmin could see the same good looks registered in the boyish face which looked smilingly back at her from within the frame.

A more recent photo had been placed among the others and although he appeared to have left his boyhood behind Tarmin could still see the likeness. A girl was standing next to him and was holding him in a propriority manner which declared to the world, 'He's mine'. She was laughing up into his face, and he, in turn was smiling down into hers. Tarmin wondered if they'd been in love or more to the point if they were still in love. She was certainly beautiful, very dainty, and perfect in every way. She wondered where this woman was now. Perhaps she was waiting for Zac to call or had she been relegated to the past. So many questions filled her mind, all of them demanding an immediate answer. There was an inscription scrawled across the bottom of the photograph which boldly stated, "To my darling Zac with love always from your Gail." Kisses followed the intimate inscription daring anyone to doubt their authenticity.

Any further thought was forestalled when Zac walked back into the room carrying two mugs of steaming coffee.

"Admiring my trophies?" he asked with a certain amount of pride etched into his masculine voice.

"Funny you should say that," Tarmin answered, pushing her turbulent emotions to the back of her mind.

"What's that supposed to mean exactly?" Zac asked flippantly as he came to stand behind her. He'd placed their coffee down on the occasional table which stood in front of the elegantly upholstered leather lounge suite.

Tarmin pointed to the photo she'd been studying. "Is she one of your trophies?"

Zac studied the photograph for so long Tarmin thought he wasn't going to answer her. He expelled his breath as if he'd been holding it in. When he did answer his voice sounded oddly flat to her ears, "No. Actually she was one of my greatest defeats. It's not always the woman who gets hurt you know. I've been meaning to get rid of this for years." Upon saying this, he picked up the photograph to study it more formally before placing it on the bookcase with the picture facing downwards.

"I'm sorry, I didn't mean to pry." Tarmin hadn't been prepared for this explanation and was momentarily at a loss for words, not knowing how to comfort him.

"You're not. It was a long time ago. Come on, our coffee's getting cold." He grabbed her hand leading her towards the large lounge where he gently pushed her down into its opulent softness.

Tarmin longed to tell him that he'd get over the hurt which still obviously plagued him, but the words wouldn't form on her lips. Instead she felt uncomfortable and wished that she hadn't accepted his offer of coffee after all.

Sipping her coffee in silence Tarmin looked around the room. Despite its lack of female ownership the furnishings appealed to her sense of rightness. This was a room where you could relax and be comfortable. She wondered if it reflected the mood of its owner and threw him a look from under her lashes. She was instantly appalled to see him looking at her. In fact, his vivid blue eyes were raking her face with a fierce intensity which left her in little doubt as to his feelings at the present time, but still she felt safe with him.

Her body reacted instantly and she felt delicious stirrings in the pit of her stomach which started to permeate throughout the whole of her being. She knew with an intense certainty that all she needed to do was beckon and she'd be swallowed up in his strong embrace.

Breathing in deeply, she felt her breath catch deep in her throat as she tried to fight the strong emotions which were surging just below the surface of her consciousness. To give in to her feelings would be disastrous.

She wasn't to know how beautiful he thought her as he rested his tormented gaze on her. He could see she was waging a battle with her emotions and thought back to the first kiss he'd stolen from her. He wanted to be able to kiss her again, but this time he wanted her to be a willing participant. Thinking along these lines was driving him crazy. He knew he was going to kiss her. She was so beautiful, so desirable.

Reaching for her, he drew her into the curve of his arm then slowly, sensuously, he brought his lips down to savour the soft fullness of her. Tarmin recognised the raw desire she saw swimming in his eyes seconds before he reached for her, but she'd been powerless to stop his advances. She knew her own eyes mirrored the desire she could see building within him.

Tarmin knew she was lost as surely as she knew her own name as soon as she felt Zac's lips touch hers tentatively at first and then with a fierce intensity when he realised she wasn't going to resist him.

She wondered briefly if he realised who it was he held in his arms or was his mind filled with visions from the past. Was she to be a substitute lover who could fill the flesh and blood requirements he needed? Her mind stopped all conscious thought as his lips continued to caress her filling her with a vibrant ache that swept everything else away. Her heart was hammering swiftly within her chest deafening her to the doubts she'd been so wary of.

Zac's mouth left her lips and started caressing the soft contours of her face and neck before inching slowly upwards to delve his tongue into the recess of her left ear sending her spinning downwards into a frenzied whirlpool of wanting such as she had never before experienced.

As if his kisses weren't enough to fill her with an unquenchable need for him, his fingers blazed a scorching trail up the length of her arm and over her shoulder. They stopped momentarily to fondle the outline of her collarbone before descending slowly to cup the firm rounded fullness of her breast. His experienced fingers sought out her taut nipple and began to caress the nubile nub with a sweet circular motion. This casual action sent a multitude of tiny shockwaves cascading throughout the entire length of her body saturating her with unchecked emotion.

Emitting a low moan of complete surrender, Tarmin arched herself towards him wanting to feel the hardness of his taut body against her own. Zac's hand left her breast leaving her feeling momentarily bereft and she uttered a low protest which he silenced with a swift kiss. "Be patient, my lovely Tarmin," he told her in a voice laced with the thickness of his own mounting desire. Within seconds his hands were tugging at her blouse making it possible for him to tenderly caress her soft curves.

Just as quickly, Zac removed her bra exposing her round, full breasts to his heavily lidded eyes which were full of unspent desire. Groaning softly he lowered his mouth to the exposed aureole taking it into his mouth and with a firmness that had Tarmin's senses reeling he started to flick his tongue against the enflamed rosy peak sending her into a flood of wanton desire.

"Oh, my god!" she purred softly arching herself against him.

His touch was turning her into a mindless fool who wanted nothing more but to join with him in the act of wanton love making. Her own touch had become more daring and her hand which had been laying passively against his hip seemed to move of its own accord to gently stroke his inner thigh while moving ever closer towards the source of his power until she was actually touching him intimately.

Zac momentarily stopped the onslaught he was delivering to her breasts as his mind registered the hesitant caress Tarmin was bestowing on him.

"Touch me," he whispered brokenly into the curve of her breast giving her permission to do as she pleased with him. He was more than ready to change their relationship from one of mere friendship to a higher plane where they would become lovers.

Had Tarmin been thinking with her head instead of her heart she might have realised the folly of the move she was about to initiate with Zac, but with his lips manipulating her as they were and her body traitorously reacting to every touch he bestowed on her she was powerless to resist. Her rational mind had deserted her and she'd become a slave to the wonderful feelings which were coursing unchecked throughout her body.

Tarmin's breath was coming in short, sharp gasps as she struggled to contain the longing which had taken possession of her body making her impatient for his caresses. She wanted him to keep touching her, wanting nothing more than to be his.

Her touch became bolder as she slowly, but firmly, trailed her fingers over him loving the hardness she found beneath her touch. She undid the buttons of his shirt before sensciously massaging his stomach and chest with the palms of her hands. She played with the soft, fine hair growing around his nipples before starting to play with them. She felt his sharp intake of breath and had the satisfaction of feeling them grow beneath her touch and become erect. She brought her mouth down to capture one of the nubs between her teeth and gently pulled at it. Meanwhile her fingers continued their exploration of his body following the growth of his chest hair as it disappeared beneath the waistband of his jeans.

Although in a state of heady emotion her mind registered the fact that he wasn't accessible to her and she started to tug at the waistband of his pants wanting him to be free for her. She whimpered fretfully against him, momentarily lifting her lips from his nipple, when her trembling fingers couldn't unfasten the clasp.

Zac emitted a groan full of raw emotion as Tarmin explored his body. He was so close to losing total control. This had never happened to him before. He'd always managed to keep a small part of his mind free, but with this woman he knew he was lost as his mind finally registered the insistent tugging at his clothing.

He moved reluctantly hating to break the contact between them for her lips had now stopped kissing him and her hands had stopped touching him. She was looking up at him questioningly with passion glazed eyes. Her lips, he could see, were wet from kissing him and he unconsciously passed his tongue over his own lips as he thought of tasting her again.

He undid the clasp of his jeans and was rewarded with a soft smile from her as she finally realised why he'd broken the contact between the two of them.

When she would have returned to her former task he told her brokenly to wait. Strong hands unfastened the waistband of her slacks before sliding down the zip that was the final obstacle to their being together. She shivered in anticipation moving into a position that would help him rid her of her slacks leaving in their place a skimpy piece of lace that acted as underwear. They covered practically nothing and Zac's breath caught in his throat as he gazed down at her.

His deep blue eyes, thickly glazed with emotion, raked over her travelling the entire length of her perfect body taking in her firm, well rounded breasts with their peaks rosy and erect from his kisses, the trim small waist and her well rounded hips before his eyes focused on the mound that hid her womanhood from him. He trailed his hand down from her breast to the softness he found there. His fingers masterfully roved over the area before moving ever so slightly to caress her now moist inner being feeling the strength of her desire for him.

Tarmin shuddered violently with barely suppressed anticipation as Zac explored her body with his scorching touch. His eyes came to rest on an elongated strawberry coloured birthmark which was usually hidden away on the lower side of her right hip. He lowered his head to gently nibble at the non-fruit.

"You're my favourite fruit," he told her when at last he raised his head to look hungrily into her passion glazed eyes. He couldn't remember another woman affecting him so completely, arousing him to such a degree that he was willing to forget all of the promises he'd made to himself. Bringing his gaze back to rest on her body he told her thickly, "You are so beautiful . . . so perfect."

As he deftly divested himself of his clothing Tarmin was treated to the sight of his wonderfully masculine body in full arousal before he quickly rejoined her on the couch. He thought momentarily of taking her into the bedroom where they would definitely have more room but his emotions had gotten the better of him. He wanted her so badly and he wanted her now. Covering her with his heated body he soon lost all conscious thought knowing that soon she would be his.

Tarmin writhed ecstatically beneath him loving the exquisite feast her hungry body was being treated too. She could feel his body nudging her and opened herself to him as she waited breathlessly for the ultimate thrust that would finally consummate their longing for each other.

Zac, she knew, would be having similar feelings to herself and she briefly wondered while still in the midst of an emotional fog why he was holding himself back. Opening her eyes she could see he had cocked an ear and was indeed listening, but to what she couldn't fathom.

The thick emotional fog which had been clouding her befuddled brain slowly started to lift and she was able to determine for herself the loud knocking coming from the front of the house. Never in her entire life had she wished any one person ill, but at that particular moment in time she wholeheartedly would have sold her soul to the highest bidder for whoever was out there to be run over by a truck.

She smiled indulgently when she heard Zac hoarsely muttering an unrepeatable curse as he slowly dragged himself into a sitting position. He dragged his hands shakily through his unkempt hair as he fought for some semblance of normalcy trying to bring his ragged breathing under control. Perhaps he should have ignored whoever was out there and maybe they'd get the message and go away leaving him free to continue his dalliance with Tarmin.

Whoever was out there had better have a darn good reason for interrupting them, Zac thought sourly as he stooped to gather up his clothes. Directing his gaze back to Tarmin he saw she was also fumbling awkwardly with her clothes. Why, he wondered briefly, did some women get embarrassed about being seen naked. Just a few seconds ago while still in the throes of consummate passion she hadn't cared that she'd been divested of her clothing. He thought she had a beautiful body and wanted nothing more than to make love with her. He thought afresh that the person who was practically knocking the door down had better have a damn good excuse. If the caller turned out to be a door to door salesman or someone coming around wanting to save his soul he'd be extremely irked to say the least. He'd enjoy slamming the door in the jerk's face. Tarmin caught him looking at her and he was amused to see a faint flush had started to stain her delicate cheeks. Impulsively he lowered his head and started to nuzzle her lips hungrily, almost tempted to ignore the constant knocking at the front door which was, quite frankly, starting to positively get on his nerves.

Chuckling softly, as he pulled his shirt over his head, he told her, "You look as if the deed has already been done, all mussed up and positively glowing. Keep the thought and I'll get rid of whoever's out there, but if you don't mind let's use the bed. There's a lot more room plus it's more comfortable."

CHAPTER THREE

||||||||||||||||||||||||||||||

Walking towards the door Zac quickly analysed his feelings for Tarmin already knowing that he cared for her a lot more than anyone else he'd ever known. He was surprised to realise that he included Gail in his analysis of the women he'd dated over the years. Usually he found himself comparing his women to her and they were usually found to be wanting in all areas. He'd thought her to be perfect, truly loving her and now he smiled exaltedly to find he was finally rid of the pain that particular journey into love had brought him.

Tarmin completely filled his thoughts. He wanted to be with her and he hoped she reciprocated his feelings in full wanting the attraction they obviously felt for each other to grow and prosper into something they could both enjoy. There was plenty of time to tell her how he was feeling; he didn't want to rush her, after all it was still early days for both of them. He was fairly certain that Tarmin returned the attraction he felt towards her. He was usually an impeccable judge of character and he would have sworn that she was not a girl to indulge in intimate dalliances unless she was strongly drawn to the man in question and hopefully, that man was himself, Zachary Coghlan. Meanwhile they could be friends. Everything would work out the way it was supposed to if he could only be patient. He smiled knowingly to himself, and was happy with the way things were working out between himself and Tarmin. He was pleasantly pleased with the world despite wanting to do away with the dumb jerk that was still knocking on his front door. Whoever it was certainly was persistent, he had to give them that.

He thought again how he would enjoy slamming the door in the jerk's face. Opening the door the smug smile was instantly wiped away from his handsome features as he recognised the person standing forlornly on his doorstep.

"Gail!" the word was torn from him as he stared open mouthed at the girl who had meant so much to him about a million years ago. Now, he just wanted her to leave so that he could go back to Tarmin, but he felt he owed her the loyalty to at least find out why she was here standing on his doorstep looking so dejected.

When it was apparent that she wanted to come in Zac found he didn't have the heart to tell her to leave. Something to do with her being an old flame, but he was quick to realise that she meant nothing more to him and was instantly gladdened. He ushered her inside telling her to go through to the lounge room where he hoped Tarmin would be fully dressed. Thankfully she was and had even been able to restore a look of respectability to her person.

Tarmin knew their late night visitor was a woman. She'd heard the soft, dulcet tones, but hadn't been able to determine the words being spoken. She was, therefore, surprised to hear Zac inviting her into the house after he'd told her only minutes before that he was impatient to re-establish their intimate union as soon as he'd gotten rid of whoever was out there.

Recognition of the other woman, seen so recently in a photograph, instantly dawned on Tarmin's face and she paled as she looked up into a pair of beautiful green eyes before looking across to Zac from whom she wanted an explanation. Why would he invite an old girlfriend into his house when they'd been so close to making love? She hoped his explanation would appease the gnawing doubts which were starting to swirl haphazardly around in her head. Perhaps upon seeing Gail again he realised how close he'd come to making a mistake with her, Tarmin. Was he now using his former lover as an escape route? Although to be fair to Zac he probably thought he owed Gail the opportunity of an audience. Tarmin was quick to realise that the other girl seemed to be distressed and in need of some reassurance if she was any judge and because of their former union she must have thought she could rely on Zac for support.

If Zac felt uncomfortable in the situation in which he found himself he was able to hide the fact very well. He introduced the two women to each other with a minimum of fuss. For a split second Tarmin thought she detected an element of concern shinning out of his clear blue eyes, but if concern had been present it was very quickly veiled. Her eyes, she knew, held a slightly stricken look plus an element of hurt she wasn't able to completely hide. Zac had been in love with this girl, still was for all she knew. Just because they'd been about to make love didn't mean that he harboured any loving feelings for her. He was a male animal and such was the male ethos that it was thought a woman, any woman, who showed a willingness to share his bed was seen to be fair game and was hunted down until the prize was won.

On the other hand this other woman was the woman Zac had been in love with. An admission he'd made freely to her, how long ago, perhaps an hour.

Her spirits fell. *Gail's photograph didn't do her justice*, Tarmin thought minutes later after the introductions had been made. She grudgingly had to admit that the other girl was stunningly beautiful. Blond curls cascaded down the length of her back and she possessed a petite figure which Tarmin would kill for. *I bet she doesn't have to practically live at the gym to keep that figure looking so pert and trim,* Tarmin thought waspishly. She couldn't compete with perfection such as this. It would be far better to back out now while she still possessed some of the tattered shreds of her dignity. Her pride was going to take a battering, but better her pride than her heart.

Tarmin was finding it hard to concentrate on the conversation which was taking place around her. She wanted to escape this ludicrous situation in which she found herself and started to rack her brains trying to think of a plausible excuse that would enable her to leave without its looking to be too conceived.

"Well," she said at last not being able to come up with a plausible reason to leave, "I think I'll call it a night. I think my travels are starting to catch up with me. I feel dead on my feet so if you will both excuse me I'll be going." To Zac she tacked on, "Thank you for giving me a lift to the party this afternoon. Your kindness was appreciated." If her words lacked warmth could she help it? She'd had enough and wanted only to escape.

Actually her head had started to pound and if she wasn't careful the persistent ache could develop into a full blown migraine of major proportions.

Excusing himself from Gail Zac followed her to the back door and out onto his verandah. It was easier for her to slip through the back hedge than to go around the block in order to reach her driveway.

"Will I see you tomorrow?" Zac asked hopefully. He'd been hoping Gail would leave so that he'd once again have Tarmin to himself. He'd noticed how reticent she'd become and knew beyond a doubt that her quietness was due to Gail's arrival. He knew he'd handled things badly, but for the life of him he hadn't known what to do. To be in this position was entirely new to him and he was at a loss not knowing how this situation should be handled.

"No. Probably not," Tarmin answered as casually as she could. She continued, "I have a few things that I want to take care of. I wasn't planning on being home for most of the day." Tarmin found she couldn't look at him as she fostered this absolute lie.

"Such as," he persisted, wanting to know what could be so important that it would stop her from seeing him. He'd be darned if he was going to give in so easily. Surely she understood that he'd felt obliged to invite Gail into his home. She didn't mean anything to him any longer, hadn't for a very long time if the truth be known.

Taking a deep breath Tarmin launched into a spiel about going to see some distant relatives who lived near the coast. Actually it wasn't a total lie for her mother had told her that they had relatives living nearby who would welcome her if she felt the need to visit them. Zac didn't need to know that her visit was borne out of a necessity to put some distance between the two of them for the present time. Anyway just because she told him she was going to visit her unknown relatives didn't automatically mean that she would.

"I see," Zac told her not really seeing at all. He tried to repress the urge to delve any further into Tarmin's flimsy excuse, for flimsy it was, for not wanting to see him. Its transparency was plainly obvious, but still he felt the need to explain his actions in the hope that she'd understand.

"Tarmin, please, let me explain. It's not what you think. I . . ." he got no further in his deliberations for Tarmin interrupted him wanting to put an end to it all.

Raising her hand, Tarmin stopped him. She didn't want to hear anymore. It was degrading that he felt he had to explain the other woman's presence in his life.

"Please don't. You don't have to explain anything. These things sometimes happen when emotions get out of control as ours did tonight. Your friend's timely arrival saved us from making a very big mistake. I, for one, am very grateful for the interruption. Had we had sex tonight it would have made our working relationship extremely awkward, to say the least. So if you don't mind I'd rather not delve into the why's and why not's of the situation and just leave well enough alone." She told him amazed that she'd been able to school her voice into such a dispassionate tone making her sound for all the world as if she meant every word. Zac would never know how the cruel words cut into her heart. She'd rather be branded a whore and suffer Zac's rancor than face the ramifications of his knowing that she cared for him.

"Sex. I thought it was a bit more than that!" he flung at her remembering how strongly her touch had affected him. He could have sworn that she returned those same feelings.

"I'm sorry about that." She said before tacking on, "Look, it's been a while for me. I got carried away . . . ."

"Really," this was getting ridiculous. The woman standing before him certainly wasn't the warm, vibrant woman he'd held in his arms earlier in the evening. He knew that now wasn't the time to delve into why she was acting this way, but he was astute enough to know that it had everything to do with Gail's untimely arrival.

———

Tossing and turning on a bed which suddenly seemed to be made from jagged rocks did nothing to help Tarmin's oppressive mood. She had to keep telling herself that her sleeplessness had nothing to do with Zac or the fact that he was probably this very minute securely wrapped in the arms of his former lover.

"This won't do!" she told herself fretfully climbing out of bed to make her way to the bathroom. Looking at herself in the large rectangular mirror which adorned the bathroom wall she wasn't surprised to see that her face bore the ravages of a sleepless night spent crying into her pillow. Her eyes were bordered by dark smudges and her usually lustrous chestnut hair hung dankly around her shoulders. Her freckles stood out plainly against the unnatural pallor of her face. She hated her freckles and wished they would disappear, but as she got older they seemed to be more pronounced. *I bet Gail doesn't have freckles,* she thought venomously and then felt a tinge of guilt for being so contrite towards the other woman. Anyway, what did it matter? Freckles or no Gail was the one sharing Zac's bed.

"No, no, no," she exclaimed vehemently to her image and actually stamped her foot in consternation. "I'm not going to care for Zac Coghlan. I'm not going to be hurt by another man who's in love with someone else. It's just not fair."

Nursing a strong cup of black tea Tarmin sat forlornly on her back verandah. She'd given up on any idea of going back to bed and had had a shower instead hoping that the hot jets of water would revitalise her sleep deprived body. The sun had not yet begun to rise, but she could see the pale pink rays of daylight fighting their way up into the eastern sky and soon she knew the sun would win its battle with the moon ousting it out of its place for yet another day. The air felt crisp and new and Tarmin breathed deeply filling her lungs with its refreshing essence knowing that this was the start of another beautiful day in nature's kingdom.

Making a snap decision she walked inside to her bedroom and grabbed a jacket along with her bag before she headed out the back door towards her garage. She silently thanked Zac for fixing the errant doors as they slid smoothly and silently open at her light touch. She'd spend the day out of doors sightseeing, but first she'd treat herself to breakfast in the park. McDonald's was always open. She'd visit them . . . if she could find them. She was thinking of her rather embarrassing sojourn from the other day when she'd become lost on a mundane trip to the coast. Oh well, there was no time like the present to get one's bearings. At least she wouldn't have a lot of traffic to contend with this time.

For the most part Tarmin enjoyed her day telling herself that if she was to work in the tourism industry, albeit the animal side of things, it would be an asset if she could give potential tourists to the area a first-hand account of the visual delights that awaited them. She was surprised that there were so many tourist destinations to visit in the Central Queensland area. She was particularly impressed with the natural limestone caves situated to the north of Rockhampton which were home to thousands of bats. She also visited an information booth on the southern outskirts of the city where she was told the Tropic of Capricorn divided the city. There was a huge spire marking the spot and the imaginary line, she knew, marked the division of the tropics at its southern most point when, during the summer months, the sun was directly overhead. It intrigued her to think that she was actually circumnavigating a geographical spot on the earth's surface when she walked around the spire.

The early hours of the afternoon saw her heading for the coast. She was determined that she'd find her way. When she was finally sitting on the beach at Yeppoon she couldn't fathom how on earth she'd missed the turnoff to the coast for the directions had been easy to follow. It was certainly beautiful here. She'd been told the island she could see in the distance was Great Keppel Island and that she could get a ferry across to the island if she so wished. It was too late to go now, but there was always next time. The ferry left from the Rosslyn Bay marina and she was interested to learn that the bay was a sanctuary for Dugongs. They were a protected species and because of this they weren't to be caught by the fishermen who moored their boats at the marina.

There were times during the course of the day when Tarmin wasn't able to push thoughts of Zac from her mind. During these times her mouth would tremble from the effort it took not to cry, but she was determined that her efforts would be successful. Even so, she was appreciative of the fact that she could shield her tear stained eyes from inquisitive stares behind the darkened lenses of her sunglasses. She didn't want to share her misery with any uncaring members of the general public.

While visiting the coast she'd phoned her mother's relatives thinking it would be nice to have a family link close by, someone she could possibly visit in the future. An answering machine received her call so she left her details saying she'd get back to them during the week.

She was able to get some good snaps of the places she visited using her digital camera. She was particularly impressed with the two waterfalls she saw at the Kershaw Gardens in North Rockhampton. She'd heard that they were man made. They were spectacular and so natural looking with the water tumbling down into an immense rock pool; the surrounding area had been planted with palms, shrubs and a number of exotic plants. *Her mother would love this*, she thought as she continued to click away getting a good range of shots. She also used her mobile phone which allowed her to make a thirty second video recording of the area which she then saved onto her phone's filing system enabling her to use the recording process again somewhere else.

Blending in with the rest of the population wasn't difficult as Tarmin enjoyed the sights, sounds, and smells of the destinations she visited. Finding some colourful 'fridge magnets which depicted landscapes of the places she saw that day Tarmin happily placed them into her holdall. She was getting quite a collection; her refrigerator was fast running out of adequate spare space but she thought they were the perfect souvenir as they were small enough to pack up if she had to move on.

She thought she'd have to ask Zac's permission to use her work computer to download these photographs and recordings to her family. She didn't think he'd mind but she felt it was only right to ask him anyway. It might be better all round if she just went out and bought a computer for herself. Then she could talk to her family any time she chose too, day or night. She could also get a video cam which would allow her to see them as well.

Tarmin resolved painfully to herself that if she was to succeed in her new job she'd have to put the last forty eight hours out of her mind and concentrate solely on the future. She was determined to push all thoughts of Zac from her mind, but she knew this was a task which wouldn't be easy when she'd be working in such close proximity to him. Anyway, if the information Laura had imparted to her was accurate she'd be spending most of her time out of doors while Zac, being the head of the company, would spend most of his day behind a desk. She would simply ignore him, making contact only when it couldn't be avoided, or if she couldn't go through Laura.

Arriving at work on Monday morning Tarmin was dismayed to find that a meeting had been scheduled and as the newest member of the team she was expected to attend. She felt excited despite herself to be starting a new job, especially one where she was her own boss, *well almost*, she chided herself.

"Zac holds these meetings every week. He's a stickler for being on top of things," Laura told her as they made their way towards the conference room, "but you'll find him to be extremely approachable in all things. He doesn't believe in interfering in areas which are outside of his expertise, although he does insist on being informed about any major decisions which could interfere with the smooth running of the park."

Laura didn't seem to notice that Tarmin wasn't taking an active role in the conversation and continued to prattle on about subjects about which she thought Tarmin should be knowledgeable.

Other members of the staff greeted her, offering her their friendship and support as they made their way towards the Monday morning meeting. In any other circumstances she would have been happy to return their greetings, but her painful interlude with Zac still hung heavily on her mind and although she returned all salutations gregariously her smile didn't quite meet her eyes which held an element of sadness which she couldn't conquer.

One man in particular, Tarmin couldn't quite remember his name, was it Noel or Neil, came up to her and placed an arm casually around her shoulders asking her if she was ready to start working for the great man and his company. He went on to tell her that he'd place himself at her disposal if she ever needed help.

Oh brother, she thought to herself, this person must consider himself to be the park Romeo. *Every park must have one*, she mused. She'd come up against his kind before. Usually once they were set straight as to the kind of relationship she was prepared to offer them they backed off and left her alone usually finding someone else to annoy. She didn't see this person as being any different.

"I beg your pardon," she answered calmly, although inside she was shying away from this man's casual attitude towards herself and the fact that he automatically thought he could place a proprietary arm around her at a moment's notice which she just as casually removed. She wasn't a prude by any means, but she also didn't want the male population to think that she was easy game for their flirtations. She wasn't about to form any attachments which would result in her having to leave if they went sour. She was more than willing to form friendships, but she definitely wasn't prepared to go any further beyond that point.

Laura came to her rescue when she told the young man, "For heaven's sake, Mike, leave Tarmin alone. The ink isn't even dry on her contract yet and you're making a move on her."

Well so much for remembering his name, Tarmin thought although she was grateful to Laura for coming to her rescue and threw her a grateful look of thanks.

Laura nodded her acceptance then said in an undertone, "Don't worry about Mike. He's really quite a nice guy once you get to know him."

Tarmin hoped her presence at the meeting wouldn't be noticed and took a seat towards the back of the room where she thought she'd be able to make her escape at the earliest possible moment at the conclusion of this morning's proceedings. Like all the best laid out plans Tarmin found hers wasn't going to work for when Laura saw where she was sitting she beckoned for her to join her at the front of the room?

"You'll never hear what's going on from way back there," Laura told her as she prepared a place for her. "Anyway, Zac will probably want to officially welcome you to the company and introduce you. How are you two getting on by the way? You seemed to be hitting it off rather well the other day at the party. He's such a sweet young man, so caring."

Tarmin's stomach had started to lurch at the thought of Zac. She mumbled an affable answer hoping that Laura wouldn't want her to elaborate on the painful subject of her nephew.

As if on cue the man in question walked through the doorway smiling greetings to everyone before apologising for his lateness.

Tarmin felt her cheeks growing hot as she looked up at him quite disturbed that his presence affected her so strongly. Vivid memories from their brief time together flashed haphazardly through her mind making it extremely hard to concentrate. Keeping up a charade of emotional indifference around him was going to be very difficult.

Drat the man, she thought somberly to herself. *This is my first day and already I'm ruing ever meeting him. I can't believe I was so stupid as to let my emotions get so completely out of control as they did. Of course he's going to think there will be a next time, what man wouldn't?*

Suddenly finding her pen to be utterly fascinating Tarmin spent the next twenty minutes staring at its fine pointed tip. Anything was better than focusing on the man who currently held everyone's attention at the front of the room. His voice held an authority which demanded complete attention and for the most part this request was carried out. She was trying to take in all that he was saying, well for the most part anyway. She was being lulled by sweet memories from when she'd been held within his strong embrace and his voice had been sweetly seducing her . . .

"Ms. Blain," an irritated voice permeated into the recess of her mind just as an elbow gave her a gentle nudge in the side letting her know that her attention was needed.

She looked uncomprehendingly into Laura's eyes wanting to know why she'd been poked. The other woman merely smiled and indicated with a turn of her head that it was Zac who had spoken to her.

Tarmin was embarrassed to have been caught daydreaming when she should have been directing her attention towards the here and now. Her pale cheeks lit up briefly as she looked up into the face of her employer. Would he be looking at her so sternly if he realised that it was he and the sweet interlude they'd shared that had been claiming all of her attention.

"Sorry to interrupt your thoughts, Ms. Blain," he told her shortly, "but I just wanted to introduce you to some of the people with whom you'll be working."

"Yes, certainly. Sorry," Tarmin responded awkwardly, knowing he must think her terribly rude to have virtually ignored him during her very first work meeting. It didn't bode well for her work ethics and she hoped he didn't think it was something she did on a regular basis. She had meant to listen, she had, but her mind had been lured away by the sound of his voice, so familiar and yet so different speaking other things to her.

All at once the meeting was over and Tarmin was secretly relieved to know she would soon be able to make her escape.

"Ms. Blain, hang on a minute will you please. I just want a quick word," Zac's voice halted her before she could make good her escape.

For a split second Tarmin thought of ignoring him, and bolting out of the door but she doubted if she could get away with it for a second time. She sent him an inquiring look which she hoped held none of the trepidation she was feeling at being alone with him. The room was now almost empty and he seemed to be in no immediate hurry to tell her why he'd stopped her. The paperwork piled up in front of him claimed his attention as he absently thumbed through a sheaf of pages adding his signature where necessary.

It was only when they were completely alone that he turned towards her, but not before calmly walking over to close the door effectively cutting off her only means of escape. He then walked nonchalantly back over to the large oval desk which dominated the conference room and perched himself on its veneered top.

"It seems the only way that I can be assured of your undivided attention is to waylay you like this and for that I'm truly sorry, but seeing how you wouldn't let me explain the other night I'm going to have my say now. After that you can do as you please."

Tarmin met his outburst with a stony silence biting her lip to stop herself from crying out in defense of her actions. She had walked to the far side of the room wanting to put as much space as she could muster between them. A small pulse had already started to throb at the base of her throat letting her know her body had no intention of responding to the 'I don't care attitude' that she was trying so hard to present to him. He disturbed her way too much.

Her nerves were stretched to breaking point while she waited for him to speak again. Couldn't he just come out and say what was on his mind and be done with it.

She didn't want to relive the humiliation and embarrassment she'd suffered by acknowledging how close she'd come to making a complete fool of herself. This was a torment which she planned never to repeat. She'd placed her heart behind an impenetrable barricade so strong and durable that no man would ever be able to break it down again, hadn't she?

Zac walked across the room to stand directly in front of her, but he refrained from touching her. His hands were hidden in the pockets of his trousers. *He's probably angry because he missed the opportunity of making love with me,* she thought then quickly dismissed the thought as being silly. A man like Zac Coghlan could probably get any woman he wanted once he set his mind to it.

Determined that she wouldn't be the one to break the stony silence that had settled around them she cast him a furtive glance and was disconcerted to find that he was looking down at her. His eyes glittered and seemed to be telling her that he hadn't finished with her yet. She was only able to hold his gaze for a second before she had to pull her eyes away. It was bad enough that her heart was hammering painfully within the confines of her chest; she'd be damned if she'd lay herself bare before him.

His fingers gripped her shoulders. "Damn it, Tarmin, look at me." His voice told her he wouldn't brook any argument from her on this matter.

Displaying a bravado she was far from feeling she asked, "What is it you want from me, Zac?"

"I want you to listen. After that the choice is yours as to what decision you make." When he knew he had her complete attention he continued, "About the other night," Tarmin tried to look away, but he held her chin firmly, anchoring her face solidly in front of him leaving her little choice but to look up into his face which was now only inches away from her own. She could smell the aromatic aroma of his aftershave and tried unsuccessfully not to breathe in its manly essence.

He started again. "About the other night, it wasn't what you thought. If you'd stayed I could have explained." His voice sounded strained even to his own ears. Damn, he was in danger of fouling this all up. He'd planned to sound so self-assured, so confident. He wanted Tarmin to understand, to believe in him. After she'd left the other night he'd been ready to kill Gail for interrupting something that for him had been a significant moment in his life. He had finally found someone with whom he was willing to make a serious commitment concerning the rest of his life. It was just that things had gotten out of hand. He hadn't planned for them to make love.

"Zac, please, the other night was a mistake. I don't want to be reminded yet again of how close I came to doing something that would only cause the both of us untold embarrassment in the future."

"Embarrassment," he belted out the single word explosively making Tarmin wince as its intensity struck her full force.

"Yes, embarrassment. I don't sleep around, Zac."

He understood only too well the implication of Tarmin's meaning. "I don't sleep around either," he told her truthfully, wondering what the hell was going on.

Standing sedately in front of him Tarmin felt she should say something else to back up her statement of defiance. She could feel the room filling with unresolved tension, but for the life of her she couldn't seem to form the words which her brain was telling her to say. She desperately wanted to tell him that she was sorry; she wanted to say so many things, but her mouth remained obstinately, stubbornly shut. Her jaw ached with the effort it caused her. She didn't have the right to accuse him in this way especially when she didn't have a solitary shred of proof.

"Tarmin, please talk to me. You're the most stubborn woman!"

Tarmin jerked her head up effectively breaking free of the grasp he had on her chin and directed her gaze into his eyes. He looked sincere enough but then what did she really know about him. She had loved Kelvin and he was now married to her sister. She needed to trust him and as desperately as she wanted to she was unable to take that final step just yet. Things between them were moving way too fast for her liking. After all, he hadn't mentioned anything about the possibility of their being together one day. She knew she was being childish, but she wanted guarantees. She was terrified of falling in love again. She had to protect her heart in the only way she knew how. She had to keep Zac at arm's length, to erect some barriers. She couldn't afford another heartache. She was attracted to him, disturbingly so, but should she tell him how she was feeling. How very scared she was of falling hopelessly in love with him. Allowing him to penetrate her defenses could destroy her for they were already so fragile it would take but a mere push to send them crumbling down around her feet.

"Tarmin," he whispered softly, "Talk to me; tell me what's wrong."

"You're making it so hard for me, Zac,"

He stared at her in dumbfounded silence before asking her simply, "How so?"

Because I don't want to get hurt, her heart screamed, but when it came to telling him she found the words so difficult to say.

"Well," he wanted to know. He was thoroughly confused. What had happened to make her change so dramatically since the last time they'd been together?

"I don't want to like you, Zac," she confessed reluctantly to him at last.

"What!" Zac exclaimed. He couldn't believe what he was hearing. This conversation was getting ridiculous. "You don't want to like me." Had he heard her correctly; had she just told him she didn't want to like him? He'd barricaded the both of them in here with the intention of telling her about Gail. He wanted to start a relationship with her; wanted to set the record straight between them. He shook his head in confused uncertainty. What the hell did he do now?

A wavering smile trembled on her lips. She brushed her tongue over lips that suddenly felt very dry before telling him, "There are so many reasons. I guess I owe you some sort of an explanation."

"I guess you do," he butted in wishing she'd come to the point. If he knew how he'd stuffed things up between them then maybe there was still a chance that he could fix things up.

"There are so many reasons," she said again haltingly not knowing where to start now that the time had come to tell him why. He'd forced her hand by confronting her this morning. She wished she had more time to think; to give some rational thought to her words.

God, or someone, was looking after Tarmin's welfare for their conversation was interrupted by someone trying to open the conference room door. When the door wouldn't budge the person on the other side started knocking. Simultaneously Zac's beeper started filling the room with noise signaling that he had a phone call coming through.

Zac threw his hands into the air and swore loudly. This was too much. What else was going to go wrong? All he had wanted was a few minutes alone with Tarmin to sort out their troubles. Was that too much to ask?

The banging on the door had turned into an angry tirade making it obvious that Zac's beeper had been heard. "Hey, come on in there, open the door. What the hell is going on in there?" This exclamation was followed by loud banging while the door knob was vigorously turned again in an attempt to open the errant door.

"I don't believe this," Zac muttered to himself. This was absolutely the last straw.

"I suggest that you tell whoever is out there that they can come in before they break down the door," Tarmin suggested totally thankful for the interruption. Now she would be able to make her escape. She was gathering her things preparing to leave, but Zac stopped her.

"Wait right there, don't move," he told her as he strode purposely towards the door.

Tarmin could hear someone apologising profusely as he was told that there was a private meeting going on. Zac then added that he would contact him when the meeting was over.

When he would have closed the door again his aunt forestalled him asking if he had seen Tarmin. She was needed in her office. Then his beeper buzzed again.

"Yes," he said resignedly to his aunt, "She's in here. I wanted to go over a few things with her before she left."

"And did you?" Laura wanted to know.

"What's that supposed to mean," he flung at her throwing caution to the wind. She was giving him an all too knowing smirk that spoke volumes.

"Nothing," she answered him before beckoning to Tarmin from the doorway. "Are you ready to come now, Dear? That's if it's all right with Zac," she added flippantly.

Both women looked at him for confirmation. Laura's eyes held a hint of mischief while Tarmin's were full of relief. She was definitely ready to leave.

As she walked past him Zac told her, "We'll finish this later, Tarmin." His voice held a note of authority and she knew without a doubt that he'd seek her out later in the day. He looked at her seeking confirmation half expecting some kind of a retort from her.

"Fine," was all she said to him as she left the room followed closely by Laura.

Zac watched her leave filled with the knowledge that he had quite possibly met the woman he would one day marry. Convincing Tarmin seemed to be the only major drawback to his plans.

Although she was kept busy, Tarmin's first day at her new job passed pleasantly. Her mind kept returning to the conversation she'd had with Zac. She knew if he wanted to see her that she was powerless to stop him so she had decided the best course of action for her to take would be to be completely honest with him. She'd wanted to be, but he'd caught her off guard with his probing questions this morning. How did you tell someone you were attracted to that you didn't want to be attracted to them because the person you had loved in the past had let you down? How did you say that you were scared, so terrified of being hurt again? She didn't think she could handle those negative emotions so soon after coming to terms with Kelvin's betrayal. She smiled ruefully to herself thinking how utterly ridiculous and stupid these thoughts sounded, but it was the truth.

Tarmin's day had been divided into office time and park time. Laura had shown her where everything was situated regarding office supplies and she'd been issued with her own email account. She promptly sent emails to her parents telling them she was finally settled and contented with her new lot in life. *Well it was mostly true.* She'd check her computer before heading for home this afternoon to see if she had any answers. With the time difference between the two countries she could never remember exactly how far Australia was in front of the United States, but she reckoned it would be Sunday afternoon over there at the moment.

She wondered what her family would be doing and felt a momentary stab of homesickness. Would her mum be cooking? Her dad would be out in the yard she was sure of that. She'd inherited her love of the outdoors from him.

Laura had arranged for someone to take her into the park for a look around. Tarmin had wanted to go by herself, but had been told it was more time efficient if she had a guide until she got to know her way around. She had to grudgingly admit this to be true and was introduced to a co-worker called Guy Fulcher. She vaguely remembered meeting him at Laura's party. He'd been friendly and easy going although somewhat quiet.

He didn't seem to mind taking time out from his busy day to play nursemaid showing her how smoothly the park operated.

Zac had purchased some small motorised vehicles. Tarmin had seen them before. They made getting around the park so much easier. It was in one of these vehicles that she and Guy now sat.

Guy turned out to be a likable companion and soon they were talking like old friends telling each other things about their past.

———

Feeling pretty pleased with himself despite not having resolved the situation with Tarmin, Zac was making his way to the canteen for coffee. He turned the corridor and immediately pulled up short frowning as he saw Tarmin up ahead. She was walking with Guy Fulcher; he hadn't known they were that friendly; he could see they were deep in conversation and were talking animatedly. He heard her laughter ring out at something Guy had said. He watched with growing dissatisfaction as she casually linked her arm through his. *She doesn't do that with me,* he thought sourly and she doesn't seem to have any problems with liking him either.

He couldn't believe how seeing them together tore at his insides. *Why can't she respond to me like that,* he thought dispiritedly as he followed them towards the canteen? He purposely held back not wanting to catch up with them. The thought of becoming an unwelcome third person in their company was galling to him and filled him with distain. He had a better way of dealing with this unwanted obstacle and smiled to himself as he started to formulate a strategy in his mind. *All's fair in love and war,* he told himself and turning on his heel he strode back to his office wanting to set his plan into motion immediately.

Tarmin and Guy ended their tour in the canteen by mutual consent and had lunch together. They were laughing about some of the pitfalls of their respective professions.

"When I was still doing my studies I had this one lecturer, he was a real son of a bitch. I don't know how he used to do it, but all of my practical training was carried out in the most bizarre settings, not once did I train in a park or a zoo."

"You're kidding. I didn't know they could do that," Guy said wanting to know more.

"I kid you not. One time I spent six weeks with a circus. I think it was meant to frighten me off, but it only added to my enthusiasm. Where else could you get firsthand knowledge about elephants, camels, lions, tigers . . . talk about being up close and personal? Do you know I nearly quit my studies and joined the circus? It was so much fun. You could be sitting here talking to Tarmin the lion tamer or the elephant girl and so on," she told him impishly before her voice trailed off as she remembered back to her years of training. She finally resumed her story telling him with renewed enthusiasm, "It makes cleaning out the monkey cages a piece of cake I can tell you. Nothing so far has come close to cleaning up after an elephant that has the runs."

"I can imagine," Guy agreed before looking at his watch, "Time to go I'm afraid. I have a report to write up before I leave for the day. It takes me forever. You are looking at the original two fingered typist." He held up his two index fingers in front of him and typed the air for effect before adding thoughtfully,

"Listen, would you be interested in going out for a meal sometime?"

She must have looked a bit disconcerted for he added, "I'm only offering friendship, Tarmin. Don't look so worried."

"Oh god, was I that obvious? I've recently come out of a rather disastrous relationship. I'm sorry, but yes I'd like that. Let me know when, okay."

Now why had she told him that and with so much ease. She hadn't felt any of the heart wrenching pain associated with telling Zac about her ill-fated relationship with Kelvin. She put it down to the fact that with Guy there was just friendship between them. She didn't have the added pull of attraction when she was with him.

"Will do, actually what about Wednesday?"

"Wednesday would be fine," she told him, adding they could work out the details later.

CHAPTER FOUR

||||||||||||||||||||||||||||||

When she finally returned to her office there was an email from Zac waiting for her. It had a receipt attached to it that she had to tick which would let him know that she had opened it. He wasn't taking any chances. *This way I can't say I didn't get the message,* she mused, *unless I actually don't open it.*

The email was short and came right to the point. He was going to come over to the cottage tonight. He'd appreciate it if she'd make herself available for a half hour or so.

The nerves in Tarmin's stomach tightened as she read the message. He meant to see her that much was obvious. It would be better to just meet him and get it over with; to let things build up between them could be disastrous and didn't bear thinking about. She hoped they'd be able to make it through the evening without there being any harsh words spoken between them. She didn't want a repeat of the other night either, but just thinking of how close they had come to making love had her nerve ends jingling uncontrollably. Her heart had started to pound within her chest and she found it difficult to catch her breath.

Damn it, she thought miserably as she tried to steady her errant breathing. *This won't do; this definitely won't do at all.* The trouble was though this man attracted her like no other before him. *Well then,* her heart asked simply, *why are you pushing him away? Why don't you put an end to this torment you're putting yourself through and give yourself to him? You know you want too. Because I want some kind of a guarantee that I won't be hurt again,* she told herself. *It's too soon, way too soon. I'm not even sure that I'm fully over Kelvin and here I am thinking about doing it all again.*

"Oh shut up," she told herself contritely.

Tarmin sent Zac a reply telling him she would be home by seven if that was convenient. Within minutes her computer emitted a loud beep telling her she had mail. It was from Zac, "Big surprise there," she muttered to herself.

His answer was concise and to the point. He told her that was fine and that he would see her then.

Tarmin was going to reply but stopped as her fingers hovered over the keyboard. *This is getting ridiculous,* she thought smiling ruefully to herself. An image manifested itself into her mind of Zac and herself having all future conversations via email. Oh dear how sad that would be never to see his smiling face or to be able to touch the hard surfaces of his wonderfully masculine body.

Her conscious thoughts instantly intervened to ask, *hey, hey, hey, if that's how you feel why are you pushing him away. Life was so complicated,* she thought miserably. "Oh, not you again," she told herself contritely, "Go take a hike."

A loud tattoo sounded at her door which had her spinning around in her chair to see who her visitor was. Surely he hadn't come seeking her out when she hadn't answered his request. Her heart had started to beat wildly as anticipation travelled across her tingling nerve ends.

"Come in," she said in a voice quite unlike her own. She found she was holding her breath as she waited for the door to open.

"Hey Tarmin the lion tamer can I come in?" It was Guy. She smiled at him affectionately not minding a bit that he was mocking her about their earlier conversation.

"Just watch it or I'll get my whip," she quipped inviting him in and directing him to a chair before asking, "So what brings you here into my humble surroundings?"

"I have to cancel our dinner appointment," he told her apologetically.

"Oh, that's too bad. Not bad news I hope." She'd been looking forward to sharing a meal with him

"No, no. Orders from above I'm afraid. I'm being sent on a scouting trip. Zac wants detailed information about some vegetation we're thinking about introducing into the park. It's my baby so to speak, so I'm off as soon as I can pack my toothbrush. We can reschedule for later in the week, okay?"

"Couldn't the information be gathered over the phone?" Tarmin asked her face solemn.

"That's what I asked, but Zac wants structured evidence. He doesn't want to be responsible for introducing a noxious weed into the country, very bad for business," Guy told her casting an irrepressible grin her way. Their eyes met and Tarmin was forced to laugh despite herself. She felt disloyal to Zac making fun of him as they were so she turned the conversation back to their original conversation.

"Oh well," Tarmin said, "look on it as a learning experience, or better still a paid holiday. Where are you going anyway?"

"Malaysia. Zac was pretty sketchy about the details. He said he'd get back to me later. It's not like him not to be well informed. He must be pretty busy at the moment."

Tarmin felt a momentary stab of guilt knowing she was probably the reason that Zac wasn't operating at full strength. It strengthened her resolve to tell him the truth about her reluctance to go out with him. She said casually, "He probably just found out. He doesn't strike me as the kind of man to let things slip through his fingers."

"Yes, well, that may be so but it doesn't alter the fact that I fly out of here first thing tomorrow with not the faintest idea of what is required of me."

Tarmin finished work for the day happy with the progress she'd made. Hopefully this evening will run just as smoothly. She'd decided to tell Zac about Kelvin. Perhaps then he'd understand her reluctance to commit herself to another relationship so soon.

"Well one can only hope," she told her reflection as she checked her appearance in her bedroom mirror a few hours later. She had opted for a casual look and was wearing a pair of favourite blue jeans and a waist length t-shirt. After all this isn't a date it's more of a clearing the air meeting.

A short time later Tarmin answered a knock at her back door and as expected it was Zac who stood there waiting to be ushered in.

Tarmin asked him would he like some coffee; he said no. They sounded so stilted with each other; so cautious of starting the conversation that obviously lay so heavily on both of their minds.

Looking across the room Tarmin threw him an unguarded glance smiling sheepishly at the awkwardness of the situation. She was disconcerted when he didn't smile back. *If I didn't know any better I'd say he was nervous,* she thought then dismissed the idea as being stupid. He was probably waiting for her to start talking; to tell him why she'd decided not to continue their relationship. Hell, she hadn't wanted to start one in the first place.

"For heaven's sake, Zac, say something. This is driving me crazy," she blurted out when she was no longer able to stand the silence that was lengthening between them.

"And say what?" he offered, "that I'm totally in the dark about what's happened between us since the other night."

"That would do for starters," she told him.

"Possibly, but I think the floor is yours," Zac said with a finality etched into his voice that even after such a short acquaintance Tarmin knew not to breach.

Clearing her throat she said, "Come into the lounge room. If I'm going to be crucified I might as well be comfortable," but as soon as they were seated she was on her feet again finding she had way too much nervous energy all of a sudden making it impossible for her to stay in one place. She began pacing the room trying to think of where to start this bizarre conversation.

Turning to face him she almost threw the words at him as she started to speak. "Like I said this morning, Zac, you're making it very hard for me."

"How so?" he wanted to know.

Taking a deep breath to fortify herself Tarmin hoped she wasn't going to regret saying these things to him. Fate sometimes had a way of throwing things back at you for no apparent reason other than it could. She had no assurances from him and therefore could be putting herself into an embarrassing, most compromising position.

"I like you, Zac, very much, but I don't want to like you. Like I said this morning there are reasons."

Zac went to stand up, to interrupt her but she motioned for him to stay seated.

"Please let me finish, this is hard enough," her voice wobbled uncontrollably and she knew she was teetering on the verge of tears, but she had to get these things said to him.

"Do you remember the other day on the way to your aunt's place? You were teasing me, asking if I'd left anyone behind. I said no, but that's not entirely true. I haven't got anyone pining after me over there, at least not anymore. I did though at one time a few years back. His name is Kelvin. I loved him so much, Zac. I thought we'd end up together, married, but then he met my sister, Carrie, and that as they say in the classics was that. I gave him up; had no choice really. Blind Nelly could see what was happening between them. They both tried to hide it for my sake. They both looked so miserable. I did what he couldn't. I told him I didn't love him anymore. It was the right thing to do." She looked across at Zac to see how he was accepting the story she was relating to him. She thought he looked a bit pale. He certainly looked more serious than she'd ever seen him.

"Go on," he urged wanting her to continue. He could ask questions later but for now he just wanted to listen, to try to make sense of the turmoil she was putting herself through in trying to tell him about this other guy.

"I had to get away. I couldn't bear to see them together. I found myself hoping that they'd break up and that he'd come back to me. They were . . . are so happy," she corrected herself reliving for a moment the guilt she had felt at wanting them to part. Continuing she said, "I moved to Seattle but I couldn't forget him; couldn't stop myself from loving him. It hurt so much." Tears started to spill down her cheeks and she wiped them away with the palm of her hands. "I still feel guilty sometimes and then when Carrie had the baby I knew I had to get out. I heard about this job so I went for it and here I am. She's having another baby. I want to be happy for them, but it's so hard. Then I met you and I liked you, but I didn't want to. I don't think I can go through that pain again, loving someone only to have them leave. The other night," she told him brokenly, "I enjoyed it. I really did and if Gail hadn't turned up when she did we would have made love, but I don't want to become involved with someone who has the capacity to hurt me so soon after . . . after Kel."

She started to cry then, really cry, sinking to the floor to sit on her haunches while harsh sobs racked her body. She covered her face with her hands finally releasing the pain that had tormented her for so long.

Zac catapulted out of his chair and was beside her in an instant. Wrapping his arms around her he held her while she cried. He felt so much anger for this unknown person for hurting her so badly, but love he knew couldn't be contained within barriers. It went where and when it wanted. His own eyes he knew were moist with pent up emotion. He went over in his mind the things she'd told him. It must have cost her dearly to have told him the things she had. To relive the pain of that heart wrenching time had taken courage. He admired her so much for sharing the pain of her torment with him.

He didn't know for how long he sat holding her while she cried and he didn't care. He whispered small words of encouragement to her not really knowing if she heard him or not, but it didn't really matter. What mattered was that he was here with her holding her close to his heart. Her head was cradled into the nape of his neck.

———

"Tarmin," he said gently, thinking she'd raise her head. No answer was forthcoming. *Maybe she's feeling a bit embarrassed,* he thought, but on closer inspection he found that she had literally cried herself to sleep.

Lifting her as best he could without wanting to wake her he cradled her securely in his arms and carried her through to the bedroom where he placed her gently down on the bed.

Looking down on her he noticed her eyelids were red and puffy from crying. Her face which usually supported a healthy glow was now pale and wan making her chestnut freckles stand out against the pallor. Her beautiful red locks were slightly damp from perspiration and he gently reached down to brush a stray strand away from her face.

She looked so vulnerable having just bared her heart and soul to him and he thought she'd never looked more beautiful. It took every ounce of strength he possessed not to lie down beside her; to hold her; to protect her. She was stirring up emotions within him that he'd never experienced before. He felt like a real mongrel for having these thoughts at a time like this.

Reaching for a quilt that was folded at the bottom of the bed he gently covered her while whispering, "Sleep well, Sweetheart, tomorrow is a brand new day."

He walked out of the room and headed for the kitchen where he made himself a strong cup of coffee. His hands trembled slightly as he held the hot liquid. His mind was still trying to digest the information she'd imparted to him.

Top of the list was the fact that she liked him. That was a good place to start. He liked her as well. Hell, he more than liked her. If push came to shove he'd have to admit to being halfway in love with her already. The last thing in the world he wanted to do was to hurt her. He knew he would have to tread very carefully for he could see how very fragile her emotions were at this moment. It made him uncomfortable knowing he was partly to blame, but if he planned his strategy very carefully then he knew he could also be a part of her recovery.

He smiled as a thought struck him and looked around for a pen and a piece of paper which he found on the coffee table near the phone. Settling down in one of the cottage's comfortable lounge chairs he started to write.

———

When Tarmin awoke a few hours later she was slightly disorientated even though her surroundings were familiar to her. She couldn't remember going to bed, but she was in bed. The last thing she remembered was being in the lounge room with Zac telling him about Kelvin. Her face grew hot as she remembered how she'd collapsed in a heap on the floor. Zac had held her and she remembered feeling safe closeted within the security of his embrace.

She felt strangely refreshed having released her pent up emotions. She had needed to cry; to rid herself of her love for Kelvin. She hadn't allowed herself to cry over him in almost three years.

I must have fallen asleep in Zac's arms. He must have put me to bed, she thought hazily as she swung her legs over the side of the bed and got unsteadily to her feet. She wondered if he'd stayed or had he left as soon as he put her to bed? She saw that the lights were on, but that didn't mean anything. *The only way to find out for sure is to go out there,* she told herself. She hesitantly made her way towards the lounge sure that she'd be greeted by an empty room.

She felt completely washed out and would have liked nothing better than to go back to bed, curl up and go back to sleep, but she had to satisfy her curiosity as to whether he'd stayed or run for his life.

Standing uncertainly in the doorway which led to the lounge room she spied him sitting in one of the lounge chairs. He'd removed his shoes and his long, lanky legs, casually crossed at the ankles, were propped up on the coffee table. He looked perfectly at ease, as if he belonged there. His dark blond hair was slightly ruffled standing on end in some places looking like his fingers had been raked through it several times. She felt decidedly foolish and slightly embarrassed not really knowing what to say to him. What did you say to someone to whom you had poured out your lovelorn heart and then to top it off you had collapsed on him into the bargain. *I'm sure to have used up all of my chances with this man,* she thought sadly. *He's probably thinking he's had a lucky escape, but I guess he's not the kind of man to run off. He probably just wanted to make sure I was okay before he left. He will most certainly leave now. It's a pity I didn't realise what kind of a man he was sooner.* Her heart started to pound at the sight of him sitting there waiting for her while her stomach contracted as her nerves played havoc with her already heightened senses.

"Zac," the word croaked softly out of her mouth and she cleared her throat preparing to speak again.

Zac turned having heard her call him. He could see that a bit of colour had returned to her pale features. She looked so unsure of herself, almost like she was going to cry again. He had to stop himself from going over to her and hugging the life out of her.

"Hey, feeling a bit better now," he asked in a low husky voice that held none of the emotion he was feeling. He hoped that she didn't mind that he had stayed. His reasons had been two fold. Firstly, he'd wanted to make sure she was okay when she awoke for she had put herself through hell tonight. If she had slept the night through he would have slept on the floor. Secondly, he wanted to address the issues she'd raised which concerned him. He wanted to set the record straight between them on that score at least. Then it was up to her as to what would happen between them.

"Barely," she told him truthfully. Her voice was hardly more than a whisper as she advanced further into the room stopping just short of where he sat. She was defensively hugging herself with her arms barred across her chest. Stray locks of her hair had fallen across her face and she feebly pushed them back behind her ears.

"Zac, I'm so sorry for tonight. I never meant to . . . ," she faltered as she tried to find the right words, "I only wanted to explain to you about Kelvin. What must you think of me carrying on like that?" Fresh tears pricked at her eyelids and her voice wobbled slightly with the effort it took to hold them at bay.

"I think it took a hell of a lot of guts. I don't know if I could have done it, but I'm really glad that you did," he told her honestly. He was extremely proud of her for having the courage to tell him her innermost feelings regardless of whether she'd meant to or not. That meant nothing. She'd laid herself bare to him tonight. He then added, "It's helped me to better understand the person you are, Ms. Tarmin Elizabeth Blain. I now know a little bit more about what makes you tick and I like what I see more than ever." His thoughts momentarily returned to her C.V. He felt he now understood that unflattering photo which had accompanied her work experience details. She'd been hiding herself behind a façade, and probably hadn't wanted to bare her heart to the world lest it would be trampled again. Hopefully tonight she'd rid herself of all vestiges of her other life that had hurt her so terribly. Hopefully, now she was ready to move on.

"Then you're a fool," she told him with just the smallest bit of her old spirit returning.

"No, I just know quality when I see it. If I was to let it slip through my fingers then I'd be a fool."

Tarmin stood transfixed to the spot momentarily nonplused by the turn their conversation was taking.

"Yes, well," was all she could come up with to answer him. "I could really use a cup of coffee," she added to no one in particular and would have made her way to the kitchen had Zac not forestalled her telling her to sit down saying that he'd make them both a cup.

"Did you eat anything before I came over?" he wanted to know as he made their coffee.

"No, but I'm not hungry. I could use a couple of headache pills though. You'll find some in the top drawer next to the fridge."

Zac obediently brought two small tablets out to her and placed them into her hand before handing her a glass of water to wash them down with. He waited while she took them and then placed the back of his fingers across her forehead contenting himself that she didn't have a fever.

"I'm okay," she told him, "just the stirrings of a headache. These will do the trick." She didn't tell him, however, that she was prone to mind-blowing migraines that had the power to incapacitate her for days at a time if she didn't take precautions against them.

He nodded his compliance, took the glass from her and returned to the kitchen. Within minutes he was back carrying two steaming mugs of coffee which he placed on the coffee table in front of her before taking the seat next to her on the lounge.

He felt her body tense as their thighs touched, but he said nothing. His own body, also, was reacting to her nearness, but now wasn't the time to give in to the pleasure touching her gave him. He had to stick to the strategy he'd been working on while she'd been sleeping.

"Tarmin," he said at last putting his coffee cup back onto the table before turning to look deeply into her eyes, "we really need to talk. Are you up to it?" His voice held a silent plea which she knew she wouldn't be able to ignore.

Glancing back at him, her expression unreadable, she answered his question. "I guess so." The words floated out on a long release of breath. She knew this moment had been coming all night and although not dreading the questions she knew Zac wanted to ask she wasn't sure if she was ready to answer them either. It was probably better to talk now rather than wait, for waiting for a more opportune time would only exacerbate the problem. She didn't think her nerves could withstand the strain.

Now it was his turn to stand up and pace back and forth in front of her. "Okay, just bear with me, please. I've made a list." Upon telling her this he bent down and grabbed a pen and a piece of paper from the floor beside where he'd been sitting.

"A list," she interrupted. Why on earth had he made a list? Surely he hadn't written down all of her failings. *That would be a very long list,* she thought ruefully to herself.

"Shhh. Yes, a list of questions which require a yes, a no, or a maybe as an answer."

Tarmin looked questioningly up into his face hoping to find an explanation for this offbeat request before finally nodding her head in agreement finding she was way too weary to contradict him.

Zac launched straight into what appeared to Tarmin to be a very unusual, very bizarre line of questioning.

"Okay, let's face this logically. You said you don't want to like me, but you do, right, yes or no?"

Tarmin stared at him in disbelief while he waited for an answer. *Why had she agreed to this ludicrous line of questioning,* she thought. She felt stupid, slightly breathless and just a little bit confused.

"Tarmin," he said patiently waiting for an answer.

"Yes," she answered feeling the word had been dragged from the very depths of her being. She could feel herself colouring and hoped he wouldn't draw attention to the fact.

"Good, good," he said and his dimples creased his cheeks as he sent her a smile. "That's a good start." He put a tick in the yes column.

"Zac, please, I don't want to do this. I feel stupid," she begged him to stop this torturous charade.

"But I do. You say on the one hand that you like me yet you don't want to become involved with me. I need to have it clear in my mind or I'm going to go nuts, Tarmin."

"Fire away then," she told him resignedly.

"Do you consider me to be a friend?"

"Yes," she answered. He ticked another square.

"Could you see yourself going out with me?"

She stared at him and he stared back waiting for an answer.

"Maybe," she told him not quite truthfully for she knew that she would, but he didn't have to know that. He had a big enough ego as it was.

"Mmm," he ticked another box before asking the next question, "Do you like the idea of having sex with me?"

"Zac!" she threw at him feeling her face starting to flame as memories flooded her mind from a night not all that long ago when she'd practically begged him to take her heated body and make it his.

"Just answer the question, yes, no, or maybe."

"Maybe," she said again knowing this to be an outright lie, but she couldn't say yes, she couldn't. She had some pride. How many more of these stupid questions was she going to be subjected to?

He looked down at her, but said nothing as he flicked the maybe box. She noticed a small pulse beating at the base of his neck so her answer had obviously affected him although he opted to say nothing.

"Do you trust me?"

At last here was a question she could answer truthfully without a doubt, well almost without a doubt she had to concede.

"Yes," she told him and was rewarded with a smile that creased his cheeks into those gorgeous dimples of his. He ticked the affirmative box.

"Do you still love Kelvin?" He looked at her while he waited for an answer. The very air seemed pregnant with waiting.

This particular question took Tarmin by complete surprise. Her gaze flew to his face; she had a solemn expression plastered onto her pale features as she considered what her answer would be.

"Well?" he wanted to know when he could no longer stand the silence or the suspense of waiting. Surely the fact that she was taking so long to answer him was a positive sign, wasn't it. He found he was holding his breath.

"No," she told him at last with a confidence which surprised her. "No, I don't think I do." She smiled up at him and was rewarded by an answering smile that seemed to light up his whole face.

"Good," he said casually, but he found his heart was pounding like an over worked jack hammer within his chest. He could have jumped for the sheer joy of it. With a shaking hand he ticked no.

"Do you think I play around?"

"Do I think . . . ," she repeated dumbly not knowing how she was supposed to answer a question such as that. She didn't know if he played around. These questions were getting more ludicrous with everyone he asked. *How many did he intend asking,* she wondered wanting the whole silly episode to stop.

"Okay, maybe you don't know me well enough to answer that one," he told her recognising the dilemma he could see etched on her face. "I'll answer that one for you. I don't play around, Tarmin. I may have gone out with a lot of women but never at the same time so the answer is definitely no." He ticked no and then continued on to the next question.

"Do you think I'm currently involved with anyone?"

Tarmin's thoughts immediately focused on Gail. Was he or wasn't he involved with her? She just didn't know. If someone had asked her the other night she would have definitely said yes but if what he just said was true then her response should be no, but he hadn't provided her with a plausible explanation as to why Gail had turned up the other night. To be fair though she hadn't given him much of a chance to explain. Knowing he wouldn't leave her alone until she provided him with an answer she went with the safest answer of the three.

"Maybe," she said, releasing the word on a long drawn out sigh then quickly changed her mind saying, "No. Oh, I don't know, Zac, why don't you answer this one as well. You know the answer so much better than I do."

"You were correct the second time. The answer is no." *That is if I don't count you,* he thought to himself as he ticked the negative box, but hopefully that small hiccup would soon be remedied.

"How many more, Zac? Please tell me we're finished," Tarmin wasn't sure how many more of these insane questions she really wanted to answer. She had to grudgingly admit though that through careful planning he had gathered information that she might not have admitted to in the course of a normal conversation with him.

"Only two," he told her, "then I'll make us another cup of coffee and then I'll leave . . . I promise," he tacked on when he saw the disconcerted look she threw at him. It was decidedly a new experience for him to be leaving like this, but the stakes were high and he was prepared to wait; but not forever, definitely not forever.

Tarmin nodded her agreement. She could handle another two questions, but no more after that. She would simply refuse and he'd be powerless to stop her. She could be stubborn too when the need arose. She felt completely washed out. Coffee sounded good though.

Launching straight into the next question Zac asked, "If we started going out do you think I'd be faithful?"

Tarmin looked up at him. *The questions were certainly getting much more personal, but she had agreed to answer them,* she thought regretfully. Could men like Zac Coghlan remain faithful to one woman? Thinking back over the questions and answers she'd already given her answer to this particular question seemed fairly obvious, but still she stalled not giving him an immediate response. She faced a dilemma for if she said yes she was laying herself open to possible heartache; on the other hand if she said no she wasn't entirely sure that answer was correct either. There was really only one answer to give if she was to be completely honest with herself and him.

"Is it so difficult to give me an answer, Tarmin?" he wanted to know, disturbed that she was taking so long to answer.

She began, "Based on the little I know about you, Zac, I think it's an unfair question, like the last two, but my instinct tells me to say yes, so yes I think you'd be faithful to whoever you were with at the time."

He winced at the backhanded compliment or was it an accusation, he wasn't really sure, but he said nothing and ticked the affirmative box. His jubilation was being hard won.

"Do you want to go out tomorrow night?"

"Is that the last question or what?" she flung at him, "because if it is I really don't know."

"It's the last question," he said simply wondering why she was getting so defensive because if she didn't want to all she had to say was no.

Tarmin's mind recapped the events of the last few hours. Hadn't he taken any notice of her? Had he even heard her that his last question was to ask her out? It struck her then that the questions had all been leading up to this moment. Asking about Kelvin; wanting to know if she liked him; trusted him; desired him. She thought again about the answers she'd given him and based on those answers she knew what her answer had to be. Heaven help her if she was wrong.

Summoning up her courage she told him yes for it was going to take courage to step out into the world again especially with a man as charismatic as Zac Coghlan. He had the power to hurt her, but if she was aware of that power surely she'd be able to keep it harnessed and under some semblance of control. Baring her soul tonight had finally cleansed her heart of her love for Kelvin. It had given her the chance to realise that she probably hadn't loved him for quite a while, but she'd been so used to loving him that she hadn't been able to see past him to a better brighter future.

"Are you sure?" Zac wanted to know, "you don't sound very convincing."

"Take it or leave it then go and make me a cup of coffee," she told him inflecting a note of confidence into her voice that she was far from feeling. She knew they'd talk further, but for now she was exhausted and she hoped Zac would understand and take his lead from her. She tacked on as an afterthought, "I'm sure, but I want to take it slow, okay? No huge hedges to jump just yet."

"You have my word," he told her truthfully. He'd let her lead the dance. He just hoped he'd be able to keep his emotions leashed until she was ready to take the next step in their relationship; if she wanted to take the next step in their relationship, he corrected himself refusing to think about the consequences if she, in fact, decided to end it.

———

"Guy showed me around the park today," she told him while they were drinking their coffee.

"Yes, I know, he told me when I was speaking to him this afternoon. You seem to have made quite a hit with him. He told me he thinks you're nice,"

"Did he," Tarmin said, "how sweet."

Zac silently drank his coffee. He frowned as he brought the cup up to his lips hoping Tarmin couldn't see his displeasure.

"How long will he be away?" she asked, knowing she'd miss his friendship.

"I don't know, perhaps a week, maybe longer," *How had the conversation become centered on Guy?* "He's involved with one of the women at the park. Barbara or Betty, some name like that."

"Good for him," she told him truthfully. She wasn't interested in Guy in a romantic way, but she'd have to talk to him when he got back. She didn't want anyone to think she was trying to make a play for him. Especially this Barbara or Betty for she knew only too well how rumours could start and how easily it was to get hurt if you happened to be the woman involved.

They talked for a while longer until Tarmin tried unsuccessfully to stifle a yawn which had Zac leaping guiltily to his feet.

"Right, I should go. After all I did promise. And you need to get some sleep," he told her. Leaving was the last thing he wanted to do. He wanted to make love to her, to carry her into the bedroom to finish what they'd been denied because of Gail's untimely arrival.

Tarmin stood also, swaying slightly into him as the events of the evening started to catch up with her. She placed her hands against his chest to steady herself and felt his swift intake of breath at the casual contact between them.

He placed his hands over hers covering them completely with his own before lowering his head too lightly rest against hers. He was fighting a battle with himself; one he knew he had no hope of winning. He took a deep breath in an effort to fortify himself against his traitorous thoughts and slowly stepped away from her. He couldn't stop himself from reaching out to her to stroke the side of her face in a feather like caress.

He swallowed as he looked down into her eyes trying to fathom what was going on behind their beautiful violet depths. "Right," he said again standing back from her needing to create some space between them. "I guess I'll see you tomorrow," he added huskily as he fought his emotions.

Tarmin nodded as she ushered him towards the back door. From there he could easily slip through the hedge and onto his own property.

Watching him disappear into the darkness Tarmin came so close to calling him back. She knew it would only take the slightest effort on her part to persuade him to stay, but she needed to be sure of her own feelings before becoming involved with anyone else and that included Zac. She wanted to go over the events of this evening and those ridiculous questions he'd forced her to answer.

———

The thought of seeing Zac kept intruding into her thoughts making her day seem more colourful than it probably was. If her co-workers noticed how easily a smile came to her lips as she worked or heard her singing her own rendition of the old Australian classic, 'Waltzing Matilda' under her breath they put it down to the fact that she was happy doing her job getting the park ready for its grand opening and not to a certain male who definitely had it within his power to make her heart flutter uncontrollably.

He'd popped into her office earlier this morning asking if they were still going out tonight. He'd inquired if she had slept well and was she willing to leave their dinner destination up to him. He knew a great restaurant where they would get a nice meal, he told her as his beeper started to make its presence known. A few well chosen words berating modern technology and having a busy day ahead of him had Tarmin smiling. With this knowledge under his belt he was gone leaving Tarmin wondering if he'd been there at all.

———

After Zac had left last night, she'd made herself another cup of coffee needing to set some things straight in her mind. She'd done a complete turnabout from not wanting to start a relationship with him to agreeing to go out with him but, she admonished herself quickly, that was probably due to the fact that she no longer considered herself to be in love with Kelvin. She now felt she possessed the confidence to move on. She felt free of the pain of loving him for the first time in years.

Was it as easy to fall out of love as it was to fall in love, she asked herself for she realised that she hadn't been ready to give Kelvin up before. She'd been using him like a shield that had been wrapped securely around her heart and until now no other man had been able to penetrate her defenses. In a mere matter of days, however, Zac had slipped in beneath her radar and before she knew what had happened he'd cut through the barbed wire she'd so carefully erected around herself. Now her heart was vulnerable again; open to the searing pain that loving someone could bring. She hoped she was ready for the challenge.

She'd have to be on her guard for it wouldn't do to get love and lust mixed up. *Zac will probably never tell you he loves you,* she thought. Can you honestly say that your interlude with him the other night was a result of love or was it pure lust? *Probably a bit of both,* she told herself. It had been a while since she'd allowed a man to get so close to her; and she had definitely enjoyed his touch. Her face flamed as she remembered how easily his strong hands and mobile mouth had tantalised her, teasing a yearning response from her such as she'd never experienced before.

Deciding she'd eat her lunch out of doors Tarmin had found a quiet spot under the shade of a large, leafy gum tree and settled down. The landscape around her was so beautiful, so restive that if she was to close her eyes she could almost believe she was back reliving her childhood visiting her grandparent's farm. The tree she'd chosen to sit under was a ghost gum, so named because of its pale bark. Standing straight and tall its foliage gave her plenty of protective shade from the harsh noonday sun. Tarmin could feel the sun's warmth as its heat permeated through her making her feel contented and just a little bit sleepy. Such was the beauty of living in Central Queensland. Taking off her jacket she bunched it up and using it as a pillow slipped it under her head as she prepared to lie down on the hard ground. Raising her knees she crossed one leg over the other adding to her overall comfort.

As they always seemed to lately her thoughts turned to Zac. She resolved to ask him at the earliest opportunity about his relationship with Gail. Surely he wouldn't deny her a truthful explanation. It was the least he could do, wasn't it? She didn't think she was being nosey or even prying into matters which were none of her concern, reminding herself fretfully that if it hadn't been for Gail's untimely arrival on Zac's doorstep they would now be lovers. *Who knows,* she added to her thoughts morosely, *we might have even realised that our feelings for each other were based on nothing more that sexual frustration, lust even and once those feelings had been fulfilled we would have been able to carry on as if nothing had happened. Lust or love,* her thoughts berated her. Hadn't she indulged herself with him? Didn't that put her into the same category as Zac? A sexual predator, she didn't think so and to be honest she no longer saw Zac in that light either.

Tarmin swatted at a fly which seemed to be hell bent on annoying her peace and quiet by buzzing around her nose. She swatted again. *There, that got it,* she thought as she settled down again still not having opened her eyes. Drat the darn thing was back again! This time Tarmin swore as she took a swipe at what she thought to be the small winged creature.

"Tut, tut such language and you looked so lady like laying there." Her legs were crossed at the knees with one foot idly slapping the air. She was wearing her work clothes, khaki shorts, khaki shirt and work boots.

Tarmin's eyes were instantly wide open. Her immediate vision was filled with the man who'd been occupying her daydreams. He was sitting on his haunches not six inches from her face. She had to blink to convince herself that her mind was not playing cruel tricks on her. He held a piece of grass in his hand, obviously the fly she'd been swatting. His face was alive with mischief bringing his dimples into play while his blue eyes twinkled merrily down at her.

Hiding her confusion as best she could she said the first thing to enter her mind, "If certain people didn't scare me half to death I wouldn't have sworn."

Now that he had her attention he continued, "Well except for the boots which look very becoming in an odd sort of way . . . very erotic in fact."

Purposely ignoring the erotic jibe which had her heart pounding she told him, "Yes, well, boots are a must in this line of work. Boss' orders you know. I was actually thinking of painting some flowers on them to jazz them up a bit. There's nothing worse than boring boots, don't you think?"

"To jazz them up; boring boots," he pretended to ponder the possibilities by bringing his hand up to his chin in a thinking pose. "The mind boggles," he said at last.

"Um, I did it to my last pair of boots. It works a treat and makes you feel good, great conversation starter as well." She imparted to him somewhat glibly.

"I can only imagine," he answered dryly. He could see a whole brigade of painted work boots hitting the turf in the near future from members of his female staff if Tarmin went ahead with her proposed plan. Perhaps a memo telling staff only to use appropriate material would be prudent. He smiled down at her thinking that his life certainly wasn't going to be boring if she was to become a part of it.

Feeling at a distinct disadvantage Tarmin tried to raise herself into a sitting position. She felt overpowered by his closeness. Her body was reacting to him in the usual way. Pinpoints of pleasure were jabbing at her letting her know in no uncertain terms just how attracted she was to him. She unconsciously reached out to run her fingers through one dimpled crevice as he smiled feeling the smoothness of his skin beneath her touch. "I love your dimples," she told him softly before she realised what she'd done. She pulled her fingers quickly away feeling slightly embarrassed by the personal note she'd introduced into the conversation. She hadn't meant to touch him. It must have come from deep within her subconscious mind.

"They're a present from my mother," he told her casually, "feel free to touch them any time you want." He didn't add that her touch was sending him crazy, making him wish that they were anywhere but here. He wanted to take her into his arms and hold her tightly against his aching body. He shook his head knowing thoughts of this kind weren't going to get him anywhere at this moment in time. He didn't have the time to whisk her off and make mad passionate love to her but knowing Tarmin she'd say no anyway. *Life was so damned unfair,* he told himself releasing a long drawn out sigh.

Tarmin watched the emotion playing across his face and felt a soft glow of elation punctuated with a momentary stab of guilt for putting it there, *but he affects me the same way,* she told herself.

Summoning up her courage she told him softly, "Zac, I'm sorry. You are being so patient, so understanding and I'm being such a jerk. While we're on the subject, well sort of anyway, can I just say thank you for last night. For what you did for me, for listening and well, for everything," she finished lamely feeling acutely embarrassed breaking down the way she had.

"I was glad I was there for you . . . honest," he tacked on when he saw the look of disbelief she threw at him.

CHAPTER FIVE

Deciding it was time to change the conversation back to a more neutral subject, one that wouldn't have him pulling his hair out in sexual frustration he asked casually, "So what are you doing out here anyway swatting at flies and using bad language?"

Taking her cue from him Tarmin sent him a devilish grin before telling him she'd just eaten her lunch and that now it was time she was heading back to work for you never knew when the boss might show up wanting to check on the new girl to make sure she wasn't goofing off. She pushed at him trying to move him out of the way.

Zac stopped her by putting a hand casually on her shoulder. "I'm sure he won't mind. I've heard he's a nice enough type of fella if he's given the chance."

"Um, I've heard that too." She agreed falling in with his light mood, happy to have the conversation on a more even keel.

Giving her a comical look that had her trying to hide the smile which was trying to establish itself on her face he told her, "Don't go yet. Sit with me for a while. I don't get out in the park all that much." In one deft movement he was sitting beside her.

"I thought you were going to be busy today?" she asked wondering why he'd taken the time to seek her out.

"I am, but even busy executives have to eat," he demonstrated by putting a blade of grass between his lips and pretended to eat it, feigning a look that told her he was enjoying it immensely until Tarmin remarked idly that she wondered what had possibly come into contact with the grass before it found its way into his mouth.

Zac coughed violently then turned his head away as he spat the grass out. "Trust you to think of something like that," he retorted humourously sending her a lop sided grin that started her pulses hammering again. "Now you'll have to share yours."

"Sure. Have one of these." She handed him one of the peanut butter and jelly sandwiches which was left over from her lunch. She'd grown used to the sandwich spread while she'd lived in America and had brought a jar back to Australia with her.

Looking inside the sandwich suspiciously Zac eyed the filling with distain. "What's this?" he asked distastefully.

"Peanut butter and jelly, it's delicious. Don't be a coward, try it," she challenged.

Taking a tentative bite Zac rolled the food around in his mouth before swallowing. "I think I'd rather eat the grass," he told her handing the sandwich back to her.

"You have no sense of adventure," Tarmin responded taking a large bite out of the sandwich he'd handed back. She made a great play of eating it and finished by licking her fingers sensciously one at a time.

"Next time I'll supply lunch. A Vegemite Sanger a la Zac. There's nothing like them. I promise you'll love it," he promised faithfully while a great smirk played around his handsome features making him appear almost boyish especially with those gorgeous dimples creasing his cheeks.

"I don't mind a good Vegemite Sanger. I just might keep you to that promise." Tarmin returned his banter playfully enjoying this spontaneous interaction knowing that all too soon their respective jobs would intrude. They'd have to part company with Zac going back to his office while she had an appointment with an obstinate cockatoo named Fred who had to be taught not to bite or to utter the few choice words its previous owner had taught it to say so precisely and clearly.

It was a beautiful day made all the sweeter because Zac had sought her out. It felt like they were playing hookey and Tarmin enjoyed their sweet interlude accepting this heaven sent time out of a busy schedule for both of them.

Their conversation became light and witty, matching their mood. They were two people enjoying each other's company. They shared an unspoken agreement to steer clear of anything which might bog them down in sensual mire.

As if on cue Zac's beeper emitted a shrill sound letting him know he was wanted on the phone. He'd purposely left his mobile on his office desk, something he generally never did. It was usually his constant companion. He resented the intrusion. He'd been content sitting here with Tarmin, sharing this time with her. He felt relaxed when he was with her, well most of the time anyway. There was always a certain amount of sexual tension laying just below the surface waiting; it seemed, for just the right combination to release his growing tide of passion. For the time being he had no choice but to force his feelings to be dormant. It was a new experience for him, but he told himself he was prepared to wait. Tarmin was a prize well worth waiting for.

"Come on. It looks like my lunch break is over," he sighed regrettably while getting to his feet. He held out his hand to Tarmin helping her up while he told her simply, "Duty calls."

On an impulse borne out of a desperation to touch her Zac pulled her into a light embrace and planted a soft kiss onto her unresisting lips. "Just marking my place," he told her when she looked up at him questioningly, "See you tonight at seven."

———

Tarmin was late getting away so she wasn't at all surprised to find that hers was one of the last cars still left in the parking lot. It sat humbly next to a car of generous proportions and sleek lines which spoke volumes of unlimited money and luxury. She wondered who it belonged to.

"Never mind old girl," she told her car with feeling, patting the dashboard once she was seated, "I'll bet it doesn't go half as well as you do." Tarmin had been extremely lucky in that she'd purchased her car from a young man who'd been going overseas and had needed money in a hurry. She'd made a sweet deal over the internet. The car had been waiting for her as soon as she stepped off the plane. She'd been very happy with her purchase ever since.

Taking a quick look around the car park as she drove away, Tarmin couldn't see Zac's car among the remaining few vehicles. She'd asked him on the day of the bar-b-que why he chose to drive an old Holden when he obviously had the means to drive something far more expensive and prestigious. He'd explained how he'd picked the car up from a wrecker and had painstakingly restored the vehicle bit by bit until it looked like the shiny showpiece it now resembled.

Zac must have left on time. The thought of him beating her home to get ready for their first official date had her heart pounding at super speed. She'd better hurry herself if she was to be on time. She was looking forward to a nice long soak in the tub, but she might have to forgo that pleasure this time and settle for a quick shower instead.

She was further held up by the man who worked on the gate. He introduced himself as Joe adding she only had to ask if there was anything he could ever do for her. Normally Tarmin would have loved to stay and chat, but tonight she was on a mission. A strong male face swam before her eyes making her oblivious to everything else and she was therefore disconcerted to find that Joe had been talking to her.

"I'm sorry, what was it you said?" Tarmin asked, remembering the man who was standing next to her. He must think she was very rude.

"I only said that we're having nice weather at the moment."

"Oh. Oh, yes, we are," she answered hoping she could make her escape without being too obvious. She really wanted to get home. Time was marching on.

Driving home she chided herself for being so foolish and sternly she berated herself. One date doesn't mean he has to make any kind of ongoing commitment to you. You are the master of your own destiny. You don't need to make any man the centre of your universe, not even when that man is Zachery Llewelyn Coghlan. You are your own person with your own very distinct personality, just because you like someone doesn't mean you have to lose your own identity. *Blah, blah, blah*, she thought to herself. She'd said it all before.

Ten minutes later she was pulling into her driveway pleased with herself for having successfully negotiated her way through the homeward bound traffic. It still felt strange driving over here. She kept thinking she was on the wrong side of the road and on more than one occasion she'd nearly piloted her car onto the other side of the road only to remember at the last minute that she was in the correct lane after all.

Feeling tired, but pleasantly so, Tarmin looked lovingly at the bathtub still wishing she had the time to take a long soak before she turned on the taps to the shower. Soon she was rummaging through her cupboards looking for something presentable to wear. Zac had mentioned a restaurant, but had failed to tell her which one he'd chosen.

Should she dress casually or try to knock his socks off, Tarmin thought as her eyes came to rest on a pale cream dress that was one of her personal favourites. "This one," she told her reflection as she stood in front of the full length mirror with the dress held up against her for effect.

At exactly seven o'clock Tarmin opened the front door in answer to a loud knocking thinking how punctual Zac was. She was instantly disconcerted to see him standing before her looking like he had just crawled out of a drain. He stood on her doorstep in what surely had to be his oldest, shabbiest outfit. Her look of anticipation quickly turned to one of pure consternation as she took in the way he was dressed.

"Zac!" she exclaimed, "I thought you said we were going to eat out." Tarmin was thoroughly mixed up and to top everything off, he was grinning down at her as if she was the one who was completely mad.

"Zac?" She repeated thoroughly confused.

"Tarmin," he responded in kind as he ushered her back inside, guiding her gently by propelling her steadily with the palms of his hands which rested on her shoulders.

Once they were in the living room he directed her towards a chair where he indicated that she should sit down.

Tarmin obeyed gladly, pleased for the excuse to take the weight off her legs before they collapsed from beneath her. She was fully convinced that she was becoming involved with a lunatic and he seemed to be in no particular hurry to enlighten her as to what was going on.

"Zac," she said again, but this time there was the merest hint of a threat in her voice. She was determined to find out what had happened.

"Alright, I'm sorry. It's just that you looked so funny standing there, I decided to string you along for a bit." His strong features resisted the urge to break into a smile again, "I mean you don't look funny; hell no, you look absolutely gorgeous, but when you opened the door just now you should have seen your face," he amended quickly seeing the look of doubt starting to steal across her features. She had looked beautiful, hell, she was beautiful! Framed in the doorway as she had been with the subdued lighting behind her giving her chestnut hair fiery highlights had sent his senses soaring. He was hard put not to pull her into his arms and kiss her like he so very much wanted to do, but she was looking for explanations at this point not caresses.

He launched into the reason explaining why he'd turned up on her doorstep in this filthy state. "I've been out on an errand for my aunt actually. It took longer than I thought, then on the way home the car got a flat tyre, hence my rather grubby appearance."

Tarmin's expression was almost comical as she sat and listened to Zac's story. It appeared that late in the afternoon his aunt had received a phone call asking if the park could spare someone to check out an air-conditioning duct for a runaway snake that was using the vent as a home away from home. After a lot of crawling through the duct Zac had finally apprehended the reptile, a harmless python. The people concerned had been extremely grateful that Percy had finally been extracted from their ventilation system. Percy was now happily ensconced at the park where he'd probably spend the rest of his days being pampered and having his every whim catered too.

"A snake, I wonder how a snake got into the air-conditioning vent," Tarmin mused thoughtfully, "the poor little thing must have been scared stiff."

"Not so little. Percy was a good ten feet long and not half as scared as the people involved. They were practically hysterical. Mostly women," he couldn't help tacking on before adding, "How about you? Wouldn't you be scared if you were suddenly confronted by a rather large snake?" He'd expected Tarmin to shudder at the mention of the reptile, but she seemed to be more concerned for the snake's safety. She was certainly a strange mixture. One minute she was all women, driving him crazy with wanting her, but then he was attracted to her intelligence also. He'd seen her hold up her side of a conversation on all manner of things. He was finding out so many things about her all of which he realised he had a definite liking for.

"Goodness, no, snakes won't hurt you. They're the most misunderstood of all of God's creatures. They won't hurt you if they can help it. They're basically shy. I had to do a thesis on them for my doctorate," she realised she was probably telling him something he was already quite aware of and veered off on another tangent, "As for the people being mostly women who are scared of them, I find that to be a highly chauvinistic remark which doesn't bear listening to," she finished pinning him to the spot with one of her indigo stares which was meant to convey to him that she meant business, but it failed miserably especially since he'd reacted to her accusations by slumping his broad shoulders dejectedly while he shifted his weight from one foot to the other in an effort to appear truly chastened. The look on his face could have charmed the birds out of the trees. It certainly worked on her as he knew it would and so did Tarmin who decided to give in gracefully.

"I don't know about you, but I'm absolutely starving," he told her, "What say I go home and get changed and meet you back here in about half an hour?" Zac felt that if he didn't make a move to leave that he was in grave danger of making a move on Tarmin herself. He didn't trust himself to stay in the same room alone with her and he wasn't as sure of her feelings towards him as he would like to be. Hell, he wanted to tell her and the whole world that she was his, but it was way too soon for declarations of that sort just yet. He reasoned that if he moved too quickly he could lose the ground that he'd already gained.

"Okay, but first tell me where we're going so I can choose what to wear. To tell you the truth I'd be just as happy to grab a hamburger somewhere unless you have something else planned?" Tarmin questioned casually getting to her feet. She noticed how he backed away from her as she advanced towards him

"A hamburger sounds fine. Actually I know just the place." He started walking towards the door then turned to face her abruptly to tack on an idea that suddenly came to him, "Jeans will do, although you do look stunningly beautiful in that getup, but I think you might feel out of place where we're going."

"And that is?" she quizzed him as she followed him towards the door.

"Do you like . . ." his question was never finished because Tarmin cannoned into the back of him when he stopped to answer her inquiry.

To keep from losing her balance Tarmin had to place her hands around Zac's waist to steady herself. Well, that wasn't entirely true, she chided herself, but she did have to hold onto him momentarily to keep her balance. She felt the muscles in his back grow tense from the unexpected contact with her body as he fought to maintain some semblance of control over his tightly leashed desires.

Tarmin would have been perfectly happy to stay right where she was, with her arms around him. It would have been so easy to simply rest her head upon his shoulder, against the strength of him and simply let their passions consume them both.

Zac stepped slowly away from Tarmin deliberately schooling his features to display a calmness he was far from feeling. She would never know the effort it cost him to turn nonchalantly towards her and remove her arms from his body as if nothing had happened.

Taking her cue from Zac, Tarmin schooled her features into a casualness she was far from feeling. "Do I like what?" she asked him hoping he couldn't hear the tremor that had established itself in her voice after their close body contact.

"Ten Pin Bowling. There's a bowling alley not far from here. They serve great hamburgers. Then maybe we could have a game or two. Have you ever played?" It took all of his energy to focus on their conversation when what he really wanted to do was gather her up into his arms and let their emotions run their course. He knew she was aware of him. It would only take a casual caress on his part he was sure, so why the hell didn't he do it! The word respect hammered itself into his brain.

"Once or twice back in the States," Tarmin told him casually, deliberately playing down her answer. She'd been in a league and had actually been quite good with a personal average of around two hundred and fifty, but that had been a few years ago. Since then she'd hardly played at all. Since breaking up with Kelvin she'd stopped doing a lot of things.

"Okay, so how about it, do you fancy a game?"

"Sure, why not. I'll get changed while you go and get ready. While I'm sure I'm properly dressed for a fancy restaurant, I'd feel a bit overdressed for bowling."

"Are you trying to tell me you think I should go home and change, and here I thought I was fine? The snake didn't seem to mind." Zac sniffed under his armpits as he spoke, his tone inferring he thought he was perfectly well groomed for the occasion although he couldn't seem to stop the hint of a smile that lurked around the corners of his mobile mouth and his beautiful blue eyes shimmered gleefully as he looked down at her.

———

Within the hour they were seated at a table within the confines of the bowling alley. Tarmin looked about her with interest finding everything familiar, but different. The restaurant was elevated above the lanes giving the casual observer an excellent view of any games which happened to be in progress. The constant sound of bowling balls rolling and pins being knocked over filled the air followed by the occasional shout of joy and exuberance as a ball successfully knocked over all ten pins announcing a strike.

"Let's eat first. I don't know about you, but I'm starving," Zac told her as they looked down at the bowlers below them.

Tarmin attacked her food with gusto. Zac had been right when he'd said they served a great hamburger here. "Mmm, this is good."

"It's good to see a woman with an appetite," he told her between mouthfuls of food.

"It's been a long time since lunch," Tarmin replied licking some sauce from her fingers.

They'd barely finished eating when Zac's name was called over the loud speaker letting them know their lane was ready. Tarmin's game started off badly and she was glad that she hadn't mentioned her past score prior to starting the game. She bowled a couple of gutter balls missing the pins completely and excused herself by telling Zac that she hadn't played in a while. Although her game warmed up Zac still beat her comfortably by at least twenty points. Tarmin challenged him to another game telling him the loser had to pay for dinner.

"You're on. Did you bring enough money?" he threw at her letting her know in no uncertain terms that he agreed to the wager.

Tarmin won by a good seventy points actually beating her own average. It seemed a fitting omen when in the final frame someone unwittingly played the song, 'Show No Mercy' on the jukebox. She smiled jubilantly as she turned from watching her ball smash another ten pins into oblivion thus adding another strike to her impressive score.

Advancing towards him in a menacing manner while wiggling her fingers at him using the universal sign for money she told him, "Pay up, Buster, you've just been beaten."

"Why do I get the feeling that I've just been shafted?" Zac asked her as they started to remove their bowling shoes.

"I don't know, why?" Tarmin replied innocently knowing she'd deliberately played down her bowling ability.

"Are you a hustler?" he asked her good naturedly as they made their way to the car.

"I thought hustlers only played pool."

"So did I," Zac grumbled. Actually he'd been very proud of her. She'd received a round of applause from some other bowlers who had started to follow their game with interest. She'd broken the lane record by seven points for a female player. She'd also been approached by a number of people who had wanted her to join their league and she'd told them that she'd consider their offer and get back to them.

The drive home seemed to pass in a flash with Tarmin telling Zac things about herself that normally she wouldn't have divulged to anyone. She felt completely relaxed in his company.

The car was filled with the sound of their laughter and all too soon Zac was turning the car expertly into her driveway.

Not knowing exactly what she should expect when Zac insisted on escorting her to her door Tarmin was surprised when he leaned over to give her a chaste peck on the cheek followed by a quietly murmured goodnight before he bounded down the steps back to his car as if the fires of Hades were nipping at his heels. Standing transfixed Tarmin watched as he backed his car out of her driveway to roar away into the night. Within minutes she again heard his car's powerful engine as it steadily climbed the slight slope leading to his house.

Feeling acutely disappointed she made her way forlornly through the darkened cottage to her bedroom where she slowly got ready for bed. Her bed felt cold and lifeless as she lay beneath the covers thinking back over the nights events wishing with all of her heart that there had been a different ending, one where Zac was here with her warming her thawed heart with his hot body giving her the warmth she fervently craved from him.

Trying to settle herself deeper into her bed Tarmin tried to get comfortable. Her bed seemed to have developed lumps which she'd never noticed before.

Her thoughts were disturbed by someone knocking at her back door. It could only be one person at this time of night, her crazed thoughts told her as she threw back the covers to make her way towards the back of the house before he thought she was asleep and left. In her haste to open the door she kicked her toe on one of the lounge chairs and let out a squeal of pain which sounded unusually loud to her ears in the darkness.

She was breathless by the time she reached the door and took a moment to regain her lost composure before opening it. It was only then that she realised that, in her haste, she'd forgotten to put on a robe over her pajamas. What if it wasn't Zac standing on the other side of the door waiting for her?

In answer to her unasked query Zac's voice reached her through the darkness. "Tarmin, its Zac. Open up."

Almost in relief she flung the door open. Her heart started hammering when she saw his familiar silhouette outlined in the doorway.

"Hi. Long time no see." he told her flippantly.

Moonlight was flooding through the doorway making it possible for them to see each other clearly. *Almost too clearly*, Zac thought as his eyes were drawn to her figure. He was able to make out every feminine detail of her lovely body; he could see her breasts enticing him with their fullness. He'd left her not twenty minutes ago knowing it was the right thing to do. He knew he'd surprised her, hell, he'd surprised himself with his chaste actions. When he'd arrived home he'd sat in his car wrestling with his emotions and had noticed her light go off. Then he'd tortured himself with vivid memories of her from a night not all that long ago when they hadn't been able to finish what he'd started. He burned for her, wanted her in a way no other woman had ever made him feel. He felt more for this woman than just lust. He wanted her, yes, but not just her body. He wanted her mind as well. He wanted her to know that and having reached that decision he wanted, no needed, Tarmin to know as well.

Sitting there in his car in the darkness it had all seemed so very simple to come over here and tell her. Never mind that it was the middle of the night or that he'd be getting her out of bed. All of that hadn't seemed very important, but now that he was here, now that she was standing before him like some barefoot goddess everything he'd wanted to tell her had vanished from his mind.

Tarmin stood patiently waiting for him to explain his presence on her doorstep.

Reason deserted him as he feasted his eyes upon her delectable body. He was behaving like a starving man who was suddenly presented with the opportunity to partake of a banquet. He didn't know where to start. What if she rejected him? What if his assumptions about Tarmin caring for him were based purely on his own personal feelings? He suddenly felt confused; he didn't want to scare her.

"I'd better go. It's late. I'm sorry if I startled you by barging over like this." Damn, he felt like a stupid kid. Why did Tarmin bring out all of his protective feelings whenever she looked at him like that?

"Zac," Tarmin began cautiously as he turned to leave. She put out a hesitant hand to detain him. She was sure they both wanted the same thing, but something was stopping him from committing himself to her. Tarmin knew instinctively that she had to make the next move if their relationship was to grow.

Almost shyly, she gathered him into her arms hoping he'd recognise the depth of her feelings for him and not look upon her blatant move as the act of a wanton female whose only motivation was sex. Putting her lips lightly over his, she whispered so softly he almost didn't hear her words.

"Please stay. I want you to stay." *There, she'd said it!* Now it was up to him to take up the gauntlet she'd thrown down.

"Tarmin," Her name was torn from him; his breath was ragged as he hungrily reached for her, bringing his lips down to cover hers thereby effectively stopping any further conversation between them.

Tarmin felt tears prickle her eyes as she was swept away on an emotional tide which totally engulfed her bringing her down into a passionate, seething, surging riptide.

Raining quick hard kisses over Tarmin's face and neck Zac's lips suddenly seemed to have taken on a life of their own and he found that now he'd started kissing her he was unable to stop. She tasted so good; he made his way back to her lips while his hands reacquainted themselves with her soft supple body. He loved the feel of her beneath his hands. She seemed to fit perfectly against him. She was like a missing piece of a jig-saw that had been a long time lost, but was now found completing the picture he'd been trying all of his life to finish.

They hadn't moved from the doorway. Tarmin was wedged between Zac and the wall. It was only when his mind dimly registered that she wasn't fully accessible to him that he raised his head realising that they hadn't yet moved inside.

In one fluid movement he picked Tarmin up, kicking the back door shut with his foot as he did so and proceeded back into the darkness towards the bedroom.

Their clothes were quickly shed and were thrown just as quickly to the floor, neither one of them caring where they landed in their haste to be rid of them.

Within seconds Zac entered her thrusting himself deep into her with an urgency that would have surprised him had he been capable of rational thought at that moment in time. His mind registered a raw cry of unleashed passion but he was unable to determine which of them had uttered the primitive, guttural noise as his body gave itself up to the wild ecstasy that was erupting within him.

When he was able to speak coherently Zac told her, "I'm really sorry about that, Sweetheart, I lost control. I've dreamt for so long about how our first time would be and I literally blew it. I wanted you so badly, but that doesn't excuse me from being brutish, does it?"

"I wanted you just as badly. I couldn't have waited a second longer," she told him honestly.

"God, I can't believe I have to ask you this, but did you climax?" He felt embarrassed. He'd never lost control so completely before, but he had to know if he'd satisfied her.

He heard her soft chuckle as she raised herself up onto one elbow to look down at him in the darkness. "I certainly did, Mister Coghlan," then added on a more serious note, "We both got carried away. I guess the sexual tension that's been building between us overpowered us both. I was actually trying to think of a way to tell you I was sorry for rushing things, but I'll let you take the blame if it makes you feel any better."

"You're a true champion," he told her flippantly before adding, "How would you like to have a rerun, only slower, much, much slower this time."

"I'd love it," she answered softly, sucking in a quick mouthful of breath for his fingers had started to fondle her breast where it hung like an over ripe piece of fruit waiting to be plucked just inches from his mouth. She delighted in the way Zac handled her body. He manipulated her senses turning her into a seething mound of unreleased passion.

Zac played with Tarmin's body coaxing her, tantalising her and although the room was in complete darkness he felt he knew her from the tip of her toes, up her long shapely legs, her well rounded hips, her slim waist, her firm taut breasts and up to the very roots of her rich chestnut locks. His mouth branded her leaving a trail of ownership.

Tarmin's breathing became ragged as she fought to control the dizzying desire that was building up inside of her threatening to brilliantly explode, but still she held on stubbornly resolute refusing to forgo even a second of the pleasure Zac was bestowing on her. She'd been powerless to do anything to him and had contented herself with touching him, clutching at him, kissing his glistening body feverishly as he masterfully manipulated her.

Knowing she had finally reached her limits and that she could no longer endure the sweet pain he was subjecting her to she groped in the darkness for him and grasped him with both hands guiding him into her. He slipped easily into her silken softness forging himself deep inside her with powerful thrusting movements. Her moans of pure pleasure shattered the quietness around them and she hoped she hadn't waited too long as she felt her body start to explode around him.

She must have subconsciously tried to stop herself for she heard Zac's voice whispering hoarsely into her ear, "Let it go, Sweetheart." before she was lost, spiraling downwards into a world of unparalled sensciousness

Tarmin had never felt so sated or content as she lay in the crook of Zac's arm. She felt drowsy and strangely secure wrapped in his strong embrace as she was.

He told her, his voice still ragged, "What you do to me should be banned, do you know that?" He gently kissed the side of her face tasting the salt from her glistening body which was still damp from their torrid love making.

Strong arms gathered her up into a loving embrace; he was content at present just to hold her. Neither of them felt it necessary to speak. She absently fondled the hair on his chest, gently teasing it around her fingers loving the silky softness of it as it caressed her body. Her bed which only a short time ago had felt cold, uncomfortable and lonely now offered them both a haven where they could be warm while sharing their love.

———

Tarmin must have slept because she awoke to a most pleasant sensation, the origin of which started way down low in her stomach. She thought at first she was dreaming, that the sensation coursing through her body was the result of an erotic dream. A very erotic dream judging from the way her body was behaving. Then she remembered; she turned and saw Zac dimly outlined in the pre-dawn light. He was laying on his side; his head was cradled by one of his hands. He was watching her noting her reaction to his teasing hand. Tarmin smiled sleepily up at him loving the sight of him next to her in her bed.

When he knew he had her full attention he slowly lowered his head to her breast gently pulling at the taut bud with his teeth until he felt it respond to his insistent assault.

Arching her body towards him Tarmin felt completely wanton in her response to him. She couldn't seem to help herself. She held his head in place over her breast enjoying the exquisite sensations which had started to travel over her entire body from his expert ministrations.

———

Tarmin's job was progressing smoothly with everything seeming to fall into place. Even the quarrelsome cockatoo, Jack, seemed to be co-operating with her. He greeted her every morning with a cheery 'Hello Tarmin' now instead of swearing at her every time she ventured near to his cage. As a result he'd been allowed to sit on a specially constructed perch adjacent to his cage.

She was pleased to see an email from Guy when she opened her message folder. He'd be back in a couple of days. She had so much to tell him and was looking forward to his return.

Whenever he could Zac met Tarmin under the gum tree in the park. They had childishly christened it their tree and it was deemed to be their official meeting place. If any of the other employees realised they were seeing each other they said nothing. Laura had given her a couple of knowing glances, but Tarmin had said nothing. She would leave telling her up to Zac. If he wanted too that was. Tarmin didn't really know.

Draining the last of the coffee from her cup Tarmin pushed back her chair and got slowly to her feet while arching her back trying to relieve the stiffness she felt from sitting for so long. *Darn paperwork*, she thought irritably. She was supposed to be outside.

She found herself thinking about Zac and wondered what he was up to. He'd been called away on business and had been gone for three days and two very lonely nights. Wrestling with her feelings she was forced to finally admit that her sour mood had nothing to do with work and everything to do with Zac not being here. She was missing him and she'd discovered something else that had thrown her for a loop; something that hit her like a bolt from out of the blue. She loved him. She had known she was strongly attracted to him, but love had a tendency to change everything making her feel more vulnerable somehow, more exposed to being hurt if he didn't return her feelings. She smiled ruefully knowing that the chances of Zac returning her feelings were very slim. *Here we go again,* her heart told her.

Her thoughts were interrupted when Laura tapped on her door before walking in to sit on the only other chair in the room that didn't hold books or pamphlets.

"Hello, Dear," she said looking around her with interest, "were you about to go out?"

"Hey, Laura," Tarmin greeted her visitor with a welcoming smile then continued, "I was, but I can put it off for a while." Sitting back down behind her desk Tarmin cleared some of the paperwork out of the way as she did so.

"I just wondered how you were settling in. I've been meaning to drop in for ages now, but work keeps getting in the way. You know how it is."

Tarmin couldn't help smiling despite her mood. Laura sounded like an apologetic friend who hadn't been keeping in touch instead of a work collogue.

"That's okay, I've been pretty busy myself. My office must look like a disaster area compared to yours," Tarmin threw a guilty glance at the clutter that seemed to be growing around her on a daily basis, "I keep meaning to tidy it up, but I never seem to get around to it."

"It's fine, Dear," the other woman told her pleasantly before asking, "Have you heard from Zac?"

Tarmin felt herself colouring. *She knows*, she thought dismally. *What do I say?* Feeling flustered, but trying to sound ever the professional she blurted out, "Yes, this morning actually. He wanted to know how the tour packages are progressing that I've been working on."

Well it was true, he had asked. Before ringing off however he'd been outrageously sexy and very provocative suggesting all manner of things that could be accomplished between them over the telephone. He'd left her with a sexy chuckle ringing in her ears and a body that was full of volatile frustration. She remembered having to sit calmly for a few minutes while trying to catch her breath before mumbling something about bloody men. She couldn't however quite remove the self-satisfied smirk that had been playing over her face as she thought of him. She'd been able to suggest a couple of provocative alternatives herself that had heightened his sexual awareness leaving him frustrated at the distance between them.

"Did he," Laura said, "that's good. He likes to be kept up to date." Looking at her watch to check the time she told Tarmin, "It's lunch time. Do you fancy coming to the cafeteria and having a bite to eat? I'm meeting Gloria and Ruth. They won't mind and it will give you a chance to get to know them a little better."

Tarmin didn't have the chance to say yay or nay for Laura kept on talking taking it for granted that she'd come with her which of course she did.

Talking with the other women helped Tarmin to unwind. Her crankiness from the morning had dissolved, but she'd been left with a heavy head. From experience she knew she could be in for one of her headaches if she wasn't careful. A few tablets would help; she kept some in her desk drawer; she'd take some when she returned to her office.

The conversation was soon focused on the upcoming staff dinner which was to be held at the Leagues Club. Tarmin had received a staff memo about the event that morning.

"What do people wear to these get togethers," she asked, "is it casual or what?"

"It's mostly casual, but you can wear whatever you like," Gloria told her before launching into descriptions of what other people had worn in the past.

"I'm sure that whatever you choose to wear will look lovely, Dear," Laura added before answering Ruth's query as to whether Zac would be coming and who would he be bringing this time.

"If he's back I'm sure he'll come. After all, he was the one who set up the social club for the staff," Laura said. She then turned back to Tarmin to tell her, "People usually go their separate ways after eating and having a few drinks. Some play the pokies or Keno, some stay for the entertainment. There's also dancing for those who feel like it. It's usually an enjoyable night. The club has a bus for those who want to have a few drinks without worrying about having to drive home." She threw a gleeful glance Tarmin's way and gave her a mindful wink that had her face turning a crimson hue.

Quickly bringing a glass of water to her lips to hide her heightened colour Tarmin knew beyond a doubt that Laura knew about her and Zac. She wondered if Zac had informed her or was she just astute enough to figure it out for herself.

"Who do you think he'll bring," Ruth persisted, "who was the girl he brought last time? Was it Colleen? Is he still going out with her?"

"I don't know," Gloria threw in, "he seems to have a new girl in tow every time you see him. It's hard to keep count. I do remember that he didn't stay very long last time. Said he had some pressing business to attend to," Both Gloria and Ruth giggled together about Zac's prowess with members of the opposite sex.

"Now girls," Laura said to them, "It's really none of our business what Zac does in his free time or who he's seeing, now let's change the subject. He is my nephew after all."

Tarmin could have hugged Laura for getting everyone off the subject of Zac although she found herself wondering who Colleen was. How long had it been since he broke off his relationship with her she found herself wondering? It was a question she vowed she'd ask him when he returned.

She finally excused herself from the table telling everyone that it was time for her to get back to work. Once back in her office she made a beeline for her desk drawer and was dismayed to find that she had no medication left.

"Great," she told the empty room as she sat down wearily. With her elbows resting on the desk top she pinched the bridge of her nose with fingers that trembled slightly knowing she was in for a painful twenty-four hours or so.

"Tarmin, are you all right?" Tarmin jumped. She hadn't heard Laura come into the room.

"Not really," Tarmin answered from behind her hands.

"Don't let those silly women upset you, Dear," Laura said coming to stand by her side. She placed a comforting hand on her shoulder letting Tarmin know she understood. "I should have stopped them from saying too much. They aren't malicious really, they just like to gossip."

"Its not that, I'm afraid I'm on the verge of getting a migraine. I usually keep tablets in my drawer, but I've got none left so I'm in for it I'm afraid," Tarmin explained, holding up the empty packet of Inderal.

Laura sprang into action immediately taking control of the situation. "Right," she said, "I'll get you home or do you need to go to the doctor?"

"No, I have medication at home. What I need now is to sleep," Tarmin knew the procedure. She had suffered from migraines since she was sixteen.

CHAPTER SIX

|||||||||||||||||||||||||||||||

Once home, Laura saw her safely into bed pulling the covers over her as requested for Tarmin had started to shiver then giving her the medication she needed Laura told her not to come into work tomorrow.

"You need to be completely recovered before you come back to work," she was told kindly.

"Okay, if you're talking to Zac would you mind telling him not to phone me tonight? I'll talk to him later," she would explain her reasons to Laura later. She was too tired to go into it now. Also at Tarmin's request Laura had closed the curtains and pulled the blinds which cut off most of the sunlight that would have otherwise streamed into the room. She explained that the light only made her migraine worse.

"I'll do that, Dear, don't worry about it. Can I call in tomorrow to check on you?"

"Yes, that would be fine," Tarmin was very grateful for Laura's help, but she found herself wishing the other woman would leave. Her head was throbbing and she wanted nothing more than to sleep. Placing one of her arms across her forehead she effectively blocked Laura from her view before closing her eyes.

She heard the back door being quietly closed and thought briefly how no one seemed to use the front door including her then she knew only blackness as sleep claimed her ravaged body effectively blocking out the pain.

Tarmin awoke some time later feeling nauseous and scrambling off the bed ran to the bathroom to be sick. She noticed the room was now in complete darkness so the sun had gone down. Wanting to know the time she tried to focus on the digital clock which sat on her dressing table but found that her vision was still too blurred to properly make out the numbers. The throbbing in her head had lessened and was now a dull aching pain, a fact for which she was extremely grateful. Closing her eyes she went back to sleep knowing that in a few more hours the worst would be over.

Next morning found her sitting on the back verandah nursing a cold cup of coffee when she heard a car pulling into her driveway. Not Zac's car, her mind registered, so it must be Laura. For no one else knew where she lived. Anyway Zac was still away on business. She didn't know when she'd be seeing him again.

It was Laura and she was dressed for work. *She must be having a late start because of me,* Tarmin thought feeling a wave of gratitude towards the other woman.

"Tarmin, are you feeling better? You certainly look a lot better," Laura told her as she mounted the steps coming to sit down next to Tarmin on the wooden verandah.

"I'm fine now. Believe it or not it wasn't the mind blower it could have been. I have you to thank for that," she informed the other woman. Laura's fast thinking and action in getting her home had helped to alleviate the initial symptoms.

"I'm glad I could help. Is there anything I can do for you now," Laura wanted to know.

"No, but have you got time for a coffee?" Tarmin asked while getting stiffly to her feet, "I was just thinking of making another one when I heard your car. This one has gone cold."

"That would be lovely. Would you like me to get it?"

"No, it's okay." While moving around the kitchen getting their coffee ready Tarmin asked Laura the question that was uppermost in her mind. "Laura, can I ask how you knew that Zac and I had become friends?"

Tarmin was sent a sweet knowing smile as Laura answered, "Zac talks to me most days and lately it's been Tarmin this and Tarmin that and after seeing the two of you together at my place . . . well I just knew that he thought you were something special and I do too."

"Oh," Tarmin was lost for words. She hadn't expected to hear this. Tears sprang to her eyes and she brushed them away quickly, "but you hardly know me." She thought back to their time together at Laura's party. She didn't think that their behaviour towards each other could have sparked any sort of speculation from anyone. They had both talked to other people. It was true that Zac had stayed mostly by her side, but only to introduce her to other staff members. What was so special about that?

"I know enough. By the way," Laura said totally changing the subject, "I phoned Zac last night and gave him your message. He wasn't very happy that he couldn't talk to you in person as he was quite concerned. He said he wished he could have been here for you. He'll be home tomorrow night anyway so I suppose he'll see you then. He told me to tell you that you are not to go back to work until he's seen you. He said to make that very clear."

"But that's silly. The worst is over now," Tarmin protested, "I'll be fine after resting up today."

"Boss' orders, Dear" Laura advised throwing her a smile that said it's no good arguing the decision has been made.

"I suppose I can find something to do," Tarmin said recalling that she did have a few odd jobs to do around the place.

"Do you suffer from migraines on a regular basis," she was asked.

"Not exactly on a regular basis, no, but having said that I do get them from time to time although I haven't had one for ages but I've had a feeling over the last couple of days that one might be looming."

"Why is that, Dear?"

"Well I think the stress of uprooting myself and moving so far from my family and starting a new job triggered an episode." She didn't add that she'd been nursing a broken heart and then having met Zac had also turned her world upside down. She went on to explain that symptoms could appear days before the actual migraine hit the body, "then the actual migraine can last for days as well. In my particular case they are genetic going back a few generations. My mother gets them as well. I guess if I have children they might suffer too." Tarmin felt a pang of pity for her as yet unborn children.

They sat talking for a while longer before Laura finally looked at her wrist watch declaring, "Oh my, I have to go. I didn't realise it was so late." As she gathered her things she said, "Promise me you'll call if you need anything."

"Will do," Tarmin told Laura, watching the other woman as she readied herself to leave.

"Would you like to come over for dinner tonight with Bill and I? We would love to have you eat with us."

"Can I have a rain check? I don't think I'd be very good company just yet. I'm still feeling a bit dopey in the head. It's probably better if I rest and recharge my flagging batteries."

"Right you are," Laura surprised her by giving her a quick hug and kiss before walking down to her car where once inside she gave her a cheery wave before she backed down the driveway.

Tarmin spent most of the day resting knowing from experience that the time off would do her the world of good. Towards evening she'd ventured outside and was in the back yard refilling the bird feeders that she'd previously placed strategically in the surrounding trees so that the wildlife in the area could have a feed. A slight noise behind her made her start and alerted her to the fact that someone was there. Spinning around abruptly she overbalanced and a strong pair of arms reached out to steady her.

"What are you doing out of bed?" she was asked.

"Guy, hello it's so good to see you. What are you doing here?" The words tumbled out as Tarmin smiled up into the face of her friend. "And how did you know where I lived for that matter?" She threw him a suspicious look that told her nothing.

"I did a bit of snooping and found your address. Cause any problems?" he wanted to know throwing her an easy smile.

"Certainly not," she tossed at him, "but don't tell me that everyone knows I've been unwell?"

"Just about. Even Joe on the gate wanted to know how you were."

She remembered when Laura had driven her home yesterday Joe had been on duty, but she'd been in too much pain to talk to him.

Guy continued, "You've made quite an impact in the short amount of time you've been with us, my girl." She was told sincerely.

"That's very sweet, but I don't know why," Tarmin was quite moved by everyone's well wishes; "You're really a closely knit team, aren't you?"

Guy nodded his affirmation.

"Help me with these feed containers then we can go inside and have a cold drink or would you prefer coffee or tea?"

"A cold drink will do nicely,"

They were walking up the back steps when Guy spied Tarmin's work boots. "What on earth have you done to your boots?" he wanted to know picking one of them up in order to examine it more closely.

"I painted flowers on them as you can see. I think it turned out rather well, don't you?" she told him glibly as she also stopped to admire her handiwork. She had used her time off to paint the floral motifs all over her boots. Lovely bright coloured flowers now adorned them making them appear very decorative to her eye. She'd added a few green leaves and the overall effect looked very becoming against the original polished black leather. She had then sprayed a transparent lacquer over the finished paint job which would seal in the colours making them resistant to the weather.

"I wonder what Zac will say when he sees them."

"I told him the other day that I was thinking of doing it. He didn't seem to mind."

"You seem to have him wrapped around your little finger," she was told.

"No I don't," Tarmin defended herself against the unwanted accusation, "now can we please change the subject?"

"If you insist," he answered throwing her a wicked grin that suggested that he didn't believe her for a minute.

"I insist," but her thoughts nagged at her and after a moment's hesitation she asked, "Guy, can I talk to you about Zac. I'll understand if you would rather not. You are friends after all, but I'd really appreciate someone to talk to." She wasn't sure how he'd react to her asking for she hadn't known him very long. In the short time she had known him she knew she could count on his friendship.

Having to make a new network of friends was a major problem when you uprooted yourself and came halfway around the world to start a new life. Tarmin hadn't been in the country long enough to establish a firm base of friends and acquaintants but she thought ruefully, *you seem to have been here long enough to get yourself tangled up in a relationship with a man you hardly know.* Still there was no one to whom she could turn when she really needed to talk about things that were bothering her. She felt instinctively that Guy could be trusted and whatever she was to impart to him wouldn't be repeated.

"Sure," he answered warmly, "that's what friends are for."

Tarmin found herself telling him everything holding nothing back even telling him she thought she was in love with Zac. "But I don't know how he feels," she finished lamely looking across at her friend to see how he was processing the reams of information she had imparted to him.

Guy had wisely said nothing while Tarmin spoke letting her talk. *She'd certainly been through some tough times during the last few years,* he thought sadly to himself.

"Love can certainly knock you around when you're not the winner," he said, "or it can be your greatest adventure."

"You can say that again," she agreed.

"I can tell you that in all the time I've known Zac I've never known him to date anyone he has a working relationship with. A few women have tried, but he has always been resolute. You must be very special to have changed his mind on that score."

"Maybe he was just between women," Tarmin threw in as a joke.

"Maybe. He has taken out a lot of women. Gail knocked the sails out from under him and since then he hasn't been serious about anyone. He takes them out for a few months and then its goodbye and he moves on to the next one."

"Rather like an assembly line," Tarmin threw in.

Guy smiled then added, "I guess you're the only one who can truly know if his feelings are genuine. You're going to have to trust in your own feelings."

"I guess so, but I wish I had a magic lamp I could rub that could tell me."

"Don't we all. Are you sure you're not on the rebound from Kelvin?" Guy asked her, "It's happened to plenty of people before. They fall for the first person to come along after losing the love of their life."

"I know, but what I feel for Zac is so different to what I felt for Kelvin. It's so much deeper, so much more intense." She was forced to smile and shared the joke with him telling him how melodramatic she thought she sounded.'

"That's a good sign being able to laugh at yourself. It sounds like you've got it bad, my girl," Guy told her patting her sympathically on the knee.

"Thank you for listening to me, Guy. I feel so much better for having talked it through with someone," she told him sincerely, "I'm sorry for unloading all of my problems on you though, but I so needed to talk about all of this."

"You're most welcome and you don't have to worry for I am the soul of discretion when it comes to keeping secrets. None of our conversation will ever be repeated."

"I kinda knew that, but tell me, do you have a girlfriend tucked away somewhere who might get the wrong impression about our friendship?" She remembered Zac telling her that he thought Guy had a girlfriend. "I'd hate to have anyone thinking that I'm trying to steal you from under their very nose. I bet there are a lot of girls out there who think you're extremely hot stuff." Tarmin looked across at him for confirmation. He was really gorgeous looking with jet black hair, a great build, extremely tall with lovely brooding brown eyes. *What a great package for the right girl,* she thought.

"No, no girlfriend," he told her indifferently while smiling affectionately at her. "Tell me though is this outpouring of feelings a two way street? Can I unload some stuff on you as well or are you not up to it?"

"Unload away, my friend," she told him enjoying the camaraderie that had sprung up between them. She realised that tonight was the start of a great friendship, one that would endure for a lifetime.

Guy stayed for tea. They had toasted sandwiches and a can of coke while sitting on the back steps listening to the sounds of the nightlife scurrying about around them. When he left Tarmin hugged him warmly and gave him a heartfelt kiss on the cheek which he returned.

Later that night Zac phoned wanting to know how she was feeling. It was wonderful to hear his voice and her pulses started hammering at the thought of him. He told her how his meetings had progressed saying he was happy with the outcome.

Feeling secure enough to tell him she said simply, "Zac, I miss you so much."

She was rewarded when he answered, "I miss you too."

She went on to explain why she didn't want to talk to him before this, "The ringing of the phone would have made me sick. I was in too much pain. I asked Laura to take it off the hook."

"I thought as much. Have you been resting?" He wished he could crawl through the phone lines and grab her to his heated body.

"Yes, but I'll be glad to get back to work. I'm going to be bored if I don't find something to do," she told him.

"Rest up. I'll be home tomorrow. Are you well enough for visitors?" he wanted to know.

She could hear the sexy banter in his voice which set her pulses racing. "I'm more than ready for visitors."

"Good."

———

Tarmin was on tenter-hooks waiting for Zac to arrive back next evening. When his car finally pulled into her driveway she strode confidently down the steps to meet him. She could see he was smiling broadly as he watched her advance towards the car. Once free of the confines of the car he gathered her up into his arms and kissed her soundly on the lips folding her into a tight embrace that moulded her to his hardened body.

"Now that's what I call being welcomed home," he whispered hoarsely into her ear while striving to catch his breath. He took a step back to look down at her, but kept his hands resting lightly on her hips not wanting to break the contact between them even for a minute. He couldn't believe how much he'd missed her in three days. He'd driven straight to Tarmin's place from the airport. The cottage felt more like home to him now. The welcome she had given him confirmed that she'd missed him too.

I want this all the time, he thought to himself. *I want to know that Tarmin will be waiting for me whenever I come home every day and always.* They walked back inside hand in hand.

"Are you hungry?" Tarmin asked him when they were in the kitchen. She'd prepared a meal for them, nothing special just steak and a tossed salad. She had also nipped down to the local wine shop to purchase a bottle of red wine. She felt like celebrating, but for the life of her she couldn't have said why exactly. She'd dragged the small patio table inside from the verandah and placed it into a corner of the lounge room. She then set it with a red checkered tablecloth and had placed candles strategically around the room. She was satisfied with the overall result knowing that she'd achieved the intimate setting she'd been striving for. She just hoped that Zac would like it.

"Only for you," he answered starting to nibble the side of her neck sending delicious tingling throughout her body.

"Ooohh," she sighed as her body instantly started to respond to him. "Ooohh," she said again starting to tremble with the excitement that was racing through her body as he touched her. Her blood was pounding in her ears and her heart was thumping so loudly she thought it might burst. "That feels so good," she arched herself into him pushing him back against the kitchen bench wanting to feel the hardness of him against her heated body.

All the while something was nagging at the back of her mind, there was something she had to tell him, but now that Zac was kissing her she couldn't think coherently about anything and the thought of any message for him receded quickly into the background of her mind. She wanted him, nothing else seemed to matter.

She heard a distant ringing in her ears and for a moment or two was able to ignore it as wild riotous feelings overwhelmed her from Zac's delicious onslaught.

The insistent ringing of the telephone brought her back to her senses, but she hated having to break the intimate contact between them. She reluctantly pushed herself away from him to walk across the room on legs that weren't entirely stable to answer the blessed thing. *Then it was going to be taken off the hook for the rest of the night*, she thought irritably. "We seem to have an awful lot of bad luck when it came to telephones," she mumbled to herself before reaching for the handset. Her greeting to her unknown caller was not all it could have been and she instantly berated herself when she heard Laura's voice on the other end of the line.

"Laura, hello, I'm sorry for sounding so rude. You caught me in the middle of something," she told Zac's aunt while she tried valiantly to catch her breath and to school her aching body into behaving itself.

She rolled her eyes as she looked across at him and was disconcerted to see him smiling wickedly back at her as he watched her trying to calm her fevered body. She so wanted to run back into his arms; to be held in his strong embrace to feel again those wonderful euphoric feelings running unchecked throughout her body bringing it to throbbing vibrant life. She was watching him as he walked around the kitchen touching some things, looking at others. She was completely mesmerised by him. He stopped in front of the refrigerator and pulled a piece of paper from the door where she'd placed it earlier under a magnet. He looked across at her throwing her an inquiring glance as he held the message up to her. It read, "Condoms". Tarmin felt herself colouring as she remembered what it was that she had to tell Zac.

Her attention was claimed again by Laura who had been waiting for her to answer. "What," she said not having a clue what information Laura had imparted to her. "I'm sorry, Laura, what did you say?" She heard Zac chuckle in the background as she tried to concentrate on what Laura had been telling her. She had to turn away from him so that she could give his aunt her full attention.

She conversed for a few minutes more before saying, "Yes, Zac is here. I'll put him on."

"Condoms," he whispered as he took the telephone from her.

"Just talk to your aunt, I'll explain later," she informed him. "I made us a meal; I'll get it ready while you catch up with your aunt."

"Hey, Aunt Laura," she heard him say into the mouthpiece. He listened to what he was being told and then laughed saying, "No, we were just talking," He threw Tarmin a glance winking at her as he did so. She felt herself colouring again. *Pillow talk*, she thought dreamily thinking about his wild kisses and wondered when they'd be able to resume. His smile sent shivers up her spine. His dimples etched deep grooves into his cheeks making him look so very sexy.

"Aunt Laura wants to know if we want to go over there for dinner tomorrow night," he had his hand over the mouthpiece as he waited for an answer.

Shrugging her shoulders Tarmin said she didn't mind if they went. Again she found herself wondering if this was normal practice for Zac to take his girlfriends to his aunt's place.

Zac spoke for a few more minutes before hanging up the handset. He came to stand beside her as she cooked the steak. He ran his fingers sensuously up her arms until they came to rest on her shoulders. "It seems I have the family vote of approval where you are concerned. None of my other girlfriends have ever been invited to dinner unless I've specifically asked for it to happen."

"Laura's sweet," Tarmin said telling him how kind his aunt had been when she'd been suffering from her migraine.

"I'm glad to hear it, Sweetheart, but what I really want to know about is this," he said holding the note up to her.

"Ah, yes, the note," she went on to tell him that her menstrual cycle had been compromised due to her having been sick. "I didn't take a pill that night so I won't be safe for the rest of the month, hence the note reminding me to tell you that we needed extra protection. I wanted to make sure that I didn't forget to tell you, that's all, before we started anything." She'd known that if Zac touched her she'd be lost. Pre-warned was pre-armed after all

"So if we go ahead without them you could fall pregnant?" Somehow the thought of Tarmin carrying his child sent goose bumps hurtling across his body. He found he wouldn't mind a bit if their love making produced a child. In fact he'd love it. He'd thought before about having children and knew that one day he wanted them, but he'd never been able to put a face to the woman who would one day bear him a child until now.

"It's a possibility," she told him knowing she'd done the right thing in telling him for she'd hate herself if he ever thought she'd deliberately misled him and had fallen pregnant with an unwanted child. She didn't think she'd be able to bare the guilt of ever forcing him into a loveless relationship for the sake of their child.

"Do you have any?" he asked matter-of-factly. He usually kept some on hand but he was fairly certain that at this particular moment in time he didn't have any.

"No, do you?" she replied. She didn't keep this kind of thing on hand as a rule thinking any alternate kind of contraception was up to the man to supply if they were needed regardless of the reason.

"I don't think so, but we can go and have a look after we've eaten." He strolled out into the lounge room, stopping abruptly when he saw how much trouble she'd gone too in arranging the table and the room for their meal. "This looks really great, Honey." He folded his arms around her pulling her close and gently touched his lips to hers in a feather light kiss. "Come on, I'll help you with dinner."

Later as they sat on the lounge listening to music Zac asked casually, "Would you like to take a turn around the lounge room, my lady?"

"That sounds lovely," their bodies moved as one as they slowly swayed to the music.

Zac's head was resting on top of Tarmin's head. His hands were sensciously caressing her shoulder blades and he unconsciously pulled her tighter into his body loving the way she fitted perfectly against him. He realised yet again how content he felt being here like this with her. It was then that his mind registered that if they were to make love tonight they needed to go out to purchase some protection He sighed as he made his decision, a resolution that he could get through one night without touching her, but he'd need her help to see it through to its finality.

"We don't have to chase protection tonight." He crooned softly into her ear and then added mockingly, "If you leave me alone I can behave myself."

"But what if I don't want to leave you alone? What if I don't want you to behave yourself?" She emphasised as she started to lightly caress his ear with her fingertips. "Anyway there are other ways to please as you already know . . . ," she deliberately let her voice trail off and leaving the rest of her unspoken words to his vivid imagination she brought her lips up to his and began to nibble on him.

"Mmmm," he responded trying to think this through calmly before his hormones completely took over and Tarmin's kisses turned him into a mindless fool. "What if I tell you I have a headache?" he told her injecting a bit of humour into the conversation.

"Tough," she answered him with a total lack of compassion and then lowering her voice she added seductively, "I guess a demonstration is in order for me to convince you that my intentions are pure."

"Never let it be said that I stood in the way of pure intentions, demonstrate away. My body is yours to do with as you will." There was a mischievous gleam in his eye and his dimples were in evidence as he smiled down at her.

"That's more like it. Come with me, lie back, relax, this won't hurt a bit." She impishly tacked on as an afterthought, "and I promise I'll still respect you in the morning."

"Just remember I have a low threshold for pain," he jokingly threw in as he allowed himself to be led towards the bedroom.

Their demonstration lasted well into the night. They shared their bodies by touching each other, kissing each other, talking to each other until they lay exhausted, but replete in each other's arms. When Tarmin woke in the morning they were still entwined in an intimate tangle of arms and legs. Tarmin's hair was splayed out across Zac's chest covering him like a protective blanket.

"Good morning," she murmured sleepily nuzzling him affectionately against the side of his neck before drifting immediately back into a deep dreamless sleep.

———

Waking up again a few hours later Tarmin stretched her body lazily. Looking around for Zac she was disconcerted to find that he was no longer beside her. She glanced at her bedside clock and was shocked to see that she'd practically slept the morning away. She slipped on her dressing gown and wandered out into the kitchen. There was no sign of him, but he'd left a note pinned to the fridge telling her he'd gone to the park to pick up Rastus. He usually left him in the care of the park staff when he had to be away on business. There was also a P.S. telling her that he would call into the chemist before coming home to pick up some contraception. He had added that he hoped she'd approve of the colours he chose. She smiled sheepishly as her mind conjured up the colours of the rainbow.

She had time for a leisurely bath and was in the process of eating some brunch when he walked through the back door.

"So you finally woke up, did you?" he greeted her with a smile as he walked through the door then coming up behind her he placed a light kiss on the top of her head. "You looked so peaceful this morning that I decided to let you sleep."

"Thank you. I was so tired." She reached up behind her to lock her fingers behind his neck and pulled his head down so that she could kiss him properly on the lips. "I got your note; how is Rastus?"

"He's okay. I got the feeling that he didn't want to come home though. He's spending too much time by himself. We'll have to spend more time at my place."

"If you like," she told him. Nothing could put her in a bad mood today. The extra-long sleep she'd been able to have had totally refreshed her. "What are you going to do today?" It was Saturday and the week-end loomed ahead of them, theirs for the taking.

"I've been asked if I want to play golf tomorrow, but I'd rather spend the day with you if you have no objections." A few weeks ago he would have jumped at the chance to play golf but now he wanted to spend all day, every day with her. He thought how easily life could change. This was the woman he wanted to grow old with.

"I have no objections," she told him simply.

———

That evening Laura and Bill Green stood on the front verandah of their home waving Zac and Tarmin off as they drove away. They had just spent the evening in the company of Zac's aunt and uncle. Laura had cooked a beautiful meal and then they'd played cards, talked, and laughed uncontrollably at Bill's outrageous jokes.

Tarmin had been made to feel so welcome she was feeling a bit overwhelmed. "They're such lovely people, Zac. They remind me a bit of my own mum and dad." She heaved a deep sigh while thinking about her parents. A wave of nostalgia swept over her as she recalled their kindness to her.

"They're great," Zac agreed tacking on, "they've been like surrogate parents to me since my parents died six years ago."

There was a companionable silence in the car as Zac drove them back to Tarmin's place. Suddenly he turned to her saying, "How would you like to see some of Rocky's sights by moonlight before we go home?"

"Okay," she didn't mind where they were as long as they were together.

"Right, but first I'm going to get us a late night snack," he said pulling into a late night convenience store. "Be right back."

Minutes later he was back carrying two cans of coke and two Mars Bars. He handed the food and drink to her as he settled himself back in behind the wheel. "I have a passion for chocolate," he told her by way of an explanation.

"So do I," Tarmin confessed sending him a pathetic grin which conveyed her complete understanding of his addiction.

"You know what; you haven't lived until you've eaten chocolate under the stars and then washed it down with a nice can of cold drink."

Fifteen minutes later they were pulling into the secluded car park at the top of Mount Archer. "You get a magnificent view of the city from up here," Zac was telling her. "By day this is a picnic area, but I've been hearing that a few tourists have spotted wild pigs roaming around. There are also some walking tracks which start from up here if ever you want to take a closer look at the mountain. You probably didn't notice, but on the way up inlets have been cut into the road allowing you to get out of your car where you can also get a great view of the river."

"And by night?" Tarmin couldn't help asking.

"By night the stars come out and so do the local Romeos I guess," he answered her nonchalantly.

"You guess, don't you know?" she teased.

"Not first hand, no, but I've heard a few rumours. If the rumours are true the local lads must be taking a break tonight because we seem to have the place to ourselves," he said as he glanced around him then added casually, "Do you want to sit at one of the tables? You'll get a much better view of the city and the stars."

"It's beautiful," she told him as she sat looking down on the lights of the city before casting her eyes skywards to look at the splendour of the stars overhead. "Look there's the Southern Cross. Do you know I could never find it in the sky as a child? My sister would always have to point it out to me."

"Is there just you and your sister?" he asked wanting to know more about her family background.

"Yes, there is just the two of us. As I've already told you dad was in the Army. He probably thought two army brats was more than enough extra baggage to cart around. I know mum certainly did. We were rather a handful, I'm afraid. Not naughty exactly, but our quest for knowledge about the various places in which we lived invariably got us into hot water of some sort every so often." Tarmin had a wistful smile on her face as she thought of her sister. It felt good to be able to think of her without the constant torment which had lived within her since her sister's marriage to Kelvin.

She impulsively reached for one of Zac's hands and kissed him thanking him silently for he'd set her free from the prison she'd imposed upon herself since losing Kelvin's love to her sister.

Zac raised his eyebrows giving her a questioning look.

"You don't need to know," she told him simply.

———

They divided their time between their two houses, but Zac preferred being at the cottage liking the way Tarmin had decorated the place. He told her it had a presence, a cosiness that his home lacked. They played cards, board games, watched DVD's. They had just finished watching a romantic movie and Tarmin had been reduced to helpless tears, much to Zac's amazement, because there'd been an unhappy ending.

"Don't those people know they're not supposed to end a movie like that?" She felt silly but she'd been unable to stop herself from shedding tears.

"Hey, it's only a movie. Life's not really like that," Zac told her as he helped to wipe away the remaining traces of her tears.

"That's just the point. Life is exactly like that. People do break up; they do lose their partners; they do fall out of love and somebody always gets hurt." She thought momentarily of the pain she'd suffered when Kelvin had fallen in love with her sister, Carrie. Even Zac had lost Gail; he knew how it felt to suffer the pain of unrequited love. Had he forgotten about that? She didn't think so. Was the pain of losing someone different for a male? Did they have the capacity to just move on with their lives as if nothing had happened?

She started to think about Gail. They'd never gotten around to discussing her; she'd never been told why Gail had turned up at Zac's home. For all she knew he could still love her. There was no way of telling. Her mind shied away from these thoughts for she didn't want to be reminded of the fact that Zac might only be on loan to her. What would happen if Gail was to return; to come back into his life wanting to take up where she had left off? It was a distinct possibility and Tarmin knew the day might come when she would have to face her greatest adversary. She wondered if she would be able to walk away like she had done with Kelvin. Something told her it would be a lot harder to accomplish.

Her thoughts were interrupted when Zac asked, "Hey, where have you been? Somewhere out there pondering on the various love triangles of the world."

"Perhaps," she answered vaguely not really wanting to tell him she'd been thinking about Gail while pondering the possibilities of how she'd react if they were to resume their relationship.

"Anyone in particular?" he wanted to know. He could have kicked himself for bringing up the topic of stupid love triangles. He was sure she was over Kelvin but he supposed some memories were harder to forget than others.

"Tarmin," he urged when she didn't answer him right away.

Tarmin was unable to supply him with an answer, not really knowing what to tell him. She simply stated, "You're right. It's just a silly movie and I'm just a sook. I'm going to make a cup of coffee. Do you want one?" Upon saying this she jumped up off the couch and walked out to the kitchen where she filled the jug with water and getting two cups down from the shelf put coffee into them.

A slight sound behind her alerted her to the fact that Zac had followed her into the kitchen. She turned to glance over her shoulder to see him leaning against the wall. That quick glance was enough to tell her that he'd seen through her flimsy charade and was not fooled by it.

"Care to share?" he asked casually thinking she might need to talk about Kelvin a bit more.

Shrugging her slim shoulders as she turned towards him Tarmin made light of the situation telling him she'd started to think about home and her family wondering when she'd see them again. She pushed past him to get to the refrigerator wanting the milk, careful not to let their bodies touch

"Really?" as an excuse he thought it sucked. Did she think he was so stupid that he'd believe that age old excuse?

"I'm jealous of Gail," she blurted out before she even realised her mind had been going to form the words. She felt her face start to flame and felt even more ridiculous when she felt tears pricking her eyelids. She made the coffee completely unaware that she'd carried out the menial task.

"I'm jealous of Kelvin," he told her in return.

"Kelvin, why would you be jealous of Kelvin?" She wanted to know thoroughly confused. All thoughts of Gail had been momentarily pushed from her mind as she stared across at him waiting for an explanation.

"You got pretty upset over something just now. I thought it might be because of the stupid remark I made about love triangles making you think about your sister and Kelvin." He told her somewhat defensively not really wanting to bring up the subject lest he upset her further.

"I don't love Kelvin. You know that," she told him bluntly.

"And I don't love Gail. I thought you knew that," he returned totally confused about the whole situation that was starting to unfold between them.

"No I don't know that. You've never spoken about her to me. For all I know she could be out there somewhere just waiting to reclaim you."

"Never," he told her honestly before adding, "Why would I want to talk about her to you?"

"Why did she come to your house that night, Zac?"

Recognition dawned on him as he finally began to understand why Tarmin was acting as she was. "Oh my god, I've been such a fool. I never thought about it to tell you the truth. I'd been so busy trying to figure out why you were acting so strangely towards me even before I knew about Kelvin that I never gave Gail another thought. I thought you were kicking yourself for getting involved with me."

He pushed himself away from the wall coming to stand in front of her when he saw her look of confusion. He placed his hands on her hips drawing her close to him as he launched into an explanation about Gail.

"Gail is married, Honey. She'd had an argument with her husband, Tom I think his name is. She just needed someone to talk too. We talked nothing else. She got everything off her chest and left."

"So you didn't sleep with her then?" Even now her mind was tormented with images of the two of them. She shook her head to rid herself of the picture it presented.

"No," he told her with such incredulance etched into his voice that Tarmin felt the corners of her mouth starting to curl but forced her features to remain passive. Now wasn't the time to start smiling even if it was a smile of victory. "Don't tell me you thought I slept with her after being with you?"

She nodded not quite able to form the words she wanted to say like she was sorry for ever doubting him; sorry for tormenting herself with images of him being with Gail; images made all the more vivid because she now knew how wonderful he was; how completely he satisfied a woman's needs.

"Incredible," he said at last shaking his head in wonder as he looked down at her. He then tacked on for good measure, "Listen closely, okay, she means nothing to me. Neither do any of the women I've taken out since. Do you understand?"

"You don't have to brag," she threw at him lightly then quickly added, "Yes, I understand, but you could have told me," when she saw the look of exasperation he was giving her.

"You didn't ask. How was I supposed to know you were upset over her? I'm not a mind reader. Anyway, a gentleman never divulges such things. It's a code of honour amongst us males; an unwritten law; a . . . a . . . feel free to help me out here," he requested of her as he rambled on not able to think of anything else to add to the ridiculous line of reasoning he'd started.

"A lot of bull," she finished for him.

"That too, although I wouldn't have put it quite like that," he agreed smiling down at her then added, "So is it safe to say we can close the chapter on Kelvin and Gail and let the poor devils rest in peace?"

"That would be wonderful," she told him truthfully then added as a thought struck her, "Do you know how close we came to having our first fight?"

"And over two people who no longer mean anything to either one of us. Am I right?"

"Yes, you're right," she agreed happily throwing her arms around his neck while deeply inhaling the strong male scent of him.

"Do you want to have make-up sex?" he threw at her drawing her even closer into the hard contours of his heated body. The smile he was giving her was outrageously sexy.

"But we didn't fight," she challenged him trying to sound serious but knew she'd failed miserably. Her body had already started to feel the delicious stirrings he always evoked within her.

"Close enough is good enough," he continued with his bantering while he brought his lips down to nuzzle her ear.

"But I just made coffee." She shuddered ecstatically sucking in her breath as he continued to chew on her ear.

He picked up the two steaming mugs of coffee and tipped them into the sink telling her, "I'll make you another one later."

The smile she gave him was all the answer he needed.

"Do you want that cup of coffee now?" he asked her still feeling slightly euphoric from their love making, "I did promise after all."

"No," Tarmin purred. She was content to stay in bed securely wrapped in his arms especially since he'd started to nibble on her earlobe again reigniting the delicious sensations her body so loved. She stretched luxuriously against the length of him and immediately felt him respond as their naked bodies touched.

"No," she said again seductively, "I want to stay right here."

CHAPTER SEVEN

||||||||||||||||||||||||||||||

A few nights later they were happily ensconced on the lounge at Tarmin's place, both were barefoot, and one of Tarmin's legs was thrown intimately across Zac's lap. He was subconsciously massaging one of her feet while he read the evening paper. The television was playing in the background, but unless something caught their eye they weren't paying particular attention to it.

Tarmin was reading one of the many wildlife magazines to which she subscribed when she idly flipped to the back page. This particular magazine always had a 'Did you know' fact file that she liked to look at. She'd used the information she got from these small snippets numerous times when she'd had to take a guided tour through the park back home. It was useless information to be sure most of the time, but sometimes it opened up the lines of communication between her and the customers breaking the ice as it were.

"Hey listen to this," she said as she launched into the spiel she had before her, "It's about reindeer antlers. Did you know that in the past if you lived in Europe and you were found to have committed adultery you were given a pair of reindeer antlers that you had to display to let people know that you were an adulterer? Isn't that strange? I wonder where these odd traditions come from."

"Probably some randy old English gentleman who already has ten kids; his wife probably wants nothing to do with him so he chases the local lassies because he's got nothing better to do with his Saturday nights. Anyway, I thought you had to wear a scarlet letter and stay at home knitting," he countered, not taking his eyes from his reading.

"Who told you that?" she said laughing up at him noticing for the first time that he was massaging her foot.

"Some book I read at school, but I also saw the movie," Zac said trying to sound knowledgeable on the subject. It hadn't been his cup of tea at all.

"I think that was true as well, but I think it applied to the women of the time. The antlers though, what is it about antlers that could correspond to someone committing adultery? The mind boggles."

"Probably the virility associated with the animal. I really don't know." he told her flatly, "Get on the net and find out."

"Talking about randy old gentlemen I got a memo the other day telling me not to forget to remember that there is a staff dinner at the Leagues Club next Saturday night."

"How does that relate to randy old gentlemen?" he wanted to know eyeing her strangely. Had he missed part of the conversation?

"Oh, please don't stop," Tarmin wailed as he lifted his hand away from her foot. "I was enjoying that."

"What?" he asked totally lost.

"My foot, you were rubbing my foot." She told him waving her foot in the air.

"Was I," he shrugged and started caressing her toes. He hadn't realised he'd been doing it.

"Ah, that's better," she sighed relaxing further into her seat thinking his touch was nothing short of magic. Later she'd return the favour, but for now she just wanted to enjoy his masterful ministrations.

"You didn't answer my question," he told her needing an explanation to her weird comment.

"Oh yes, right, It's just that it made me think of the staff get togethers back home. There was this one old letch," she paused lapsing into silence as she thought of the work colleagues she'd left behind. Some of them had become good friends and she'd promised to stay in touch. She made a mental note to send some emails tomorrow while at work. She continued with her story, "It got to the stage where it was positively annoying. All of us girls had to start avoiding him because we all became targets. He'd waffle on about how good he was in bed and what we were missing by not taking him up on his offer."

"Some guys just don't know when to call it quits."

"Mm, it was sad really because he wasn't a bad sort of chap. He was just lonely like we all can get sometimes. He'd lost his wife years before apparently and never remarried. In the end we all felt sorry for him," she mused then added quickly when she saw the look he was sending her way, "but still annoying when he had you boxed into a corner."

"Yes, well, I'm the only old letch you have to worry about for the time being," he told her and lifting her foot to his mouth he kissed her toes one by one to drive home his point.

Tarmin opened her mouth to make a smart remark but Zac forestalled her by saying, "I don't want a running inventory on where they've been thank you, it will definitely spoil the moment."

"I wasn't going to say anything," she smirked up at him.

"Sure you weren't," he threw back at her.

"You can kiss my toes all you want," she placed her toes invitingly against his lips, "but first would you mind biting off the toenail on my little toe. It will save me having to do it later."

"Romance is definitely dead," he declared solemnly as he slowly removed her foot from his mouth to place it back on his lap where once again he started to gently massage both of her feet for her.

Zac waited for her to continue, thinking she would elaborate some more about the old letch from her memory, but nothing was forthcoming.

Instead she asked him, "Zac, will we be going to this staff dinner together?"

"Of course we'll be going together. Why wouldn't we?" he looked down at her wondering why she thought it was necessary to ask such a foolish question in the first place.

"I don't know; I just wondered," she told him pulling herself up into a sitting position thereby putting a bit of distance between them.

"Come over here," he asked and she found herself obediently obeying him, sliding across the short space to sit beside him, before he continued, "Okay bring me up to speed. What's going on in that beautiful head of yours?" He wondered if the gossip mongers had been busy and had related any of his past exploits to her, not that anyone had any information to relate.

He kept his private life and his working life completely separate or at least he had until now. He didn't think his aunt had been telling staff about any of the women he'd dated in the past. He'd never dated anyone from the park before so he knew there couldn't be any jealous co-workers lurking in the background anywhere. He didn't know if they'd been spotted talking to each other these past few weeks and he didn't care for he hadn't tried to hide the fact that he'd sought her out.

Tarmin shifted uneasily in her seat before telling him, "Well I just wondered if you wanted people to know that you were seeing me, that's all?"

"Seeing you, is that the same as going out in American language?" He'd been seeing her as Tarmin put it for three weeks now. He didn't care who knew.

"Are we going out?" Tarmin wanted to know because apart from going bowling they hadn't been anywhere. Well to be fair they'd gone to his aunt's place for dinner and then he'd taken her to see the lights of the city, but that didn't count. She was starting to think that he didn't want to be seen with her.

"I thought we were," although he had to admit that his behaviour concerning Tarmin wasn't how he usually treated his girlfriends. He'd taken them out to restaurants and to the theatre, showing them off in all of their finery, but he'd never shared so much of his inner self with anyone like he'd done with her. He wondered if it had anything to do with her living so close and then immediately dismissed the idea as being stupid. It wouldn't matter if she lived clear across town. He'd still want to spend every minute with her. He'd started to plan his day around her liking nothing better than to be in her company at the end of his working day; to discuss with her various things that made up his day. He found himself wondering if this was how married couples lived their lives; he found the idea appealed to him immensely. He'd love to grow old with Tarmin by his side.

"We never go out." She told him then realised that now he'd probably think she was bemoaning the fact when the exact opposite was true. She cherished the time they spent together.

"Do you want to go out?"

"No," she answered truthfully as she tried to explain her meaning to him, "Please try to understand, Zac, that's not what I meant. I love being here with you like this. Maybe I used the wrong choice of words. I don't care that we don't go out, honest. I actually prefer it. If we were in a restaurant now we wouldn't be like this. This is the real me," she placed her hands against her chest wanting to emphasise her point, "The me who doesn't have to put on airs and graces. I can be myself without having to bother about what other people think of me. I mean, look at me." She was wearing an old pair of blue jeans and one of his t-shirts; the one that had 'Save the Whales' emblazoned across the front. She was barefoot; not wearing any make-up, but she was content.

Her mind wandered back to earlier this evening. She'd been having a bath when Zac arrived. It had seemed completely natural to her to invite him to join her in the tub which he did. They'd sat there amongst the bubbles discussing their respective days. Tarmin knew she wouldn't change those moments for anything.

Zac put his arms around her then and drew her into the curve of his body. He placed a light kiss into her hair telling her softly and somewhat thoughtfully, "I understand perfectly because that's how I feel but just the same I'm sorry, Sweetheart. I've been selfish. I just wanted you to myself and although you've said you don't want to go out, we can. It's still early." He glanced at his wrist watch, "if we get a move on we can probably get a table somewhere."

"Zac, please I meant it when I said I didn't want to go out. I just wondered if we were going out," she emphasised the last bit realising how confusing she must have sounded. *Maybe I'm the selfish one,* she thought dismally to herself.

"Yes, Ms. Blain, we are going out." He confirmed and then added, "and tomorrow night I'm taking you out to celebrate. I won't take no or maybe as an answer either."

Their attention was simultaneously drawn to the television where loud music had started heralding the beginning of an episode of Happy Days; a show that had been popular in the sixties. One of the characters had just asked someone to go steady giving Zac a ridiculous idea. He just hoped Tarmin wouldn't think he was being too corny.

"In fact, let's make it official. Let's go steady." He wanted to tell her he'd do anything to make their union official.

Tarmin looked at him as if he'd lost his mind. Was this some sort of a joke but she decided to play along. "Going steady," she answered, "mmm, that takes some thinking about. It's a big step for a girl to make."

"We could start a new trend. I can see it now, couples everywhere pledging their undying love for each other."

"Everything old is new again," she said slightly amused by the whole idea, but at the same time her heart was happy because Zac had made a small step towards committing himself to her.

Zac was pleased with himself. He was hopefully letting her know without the necessity of words that he wanted more out of their relationship. He knew if it was up to him it would be a wedding ring that he placed on her finger, but he wanted to give her more time. Perhaps she wasn't ready for anything more meaningful just yet. He knew she was everything he'd ever wanted in a woman; excellent company, intelligent, a friend as well as a lover. What more could a man want he asked himself contentedly.

"Okay I guess we can go steady, but can you explain to me why I have suddenly developed this overwhelming desire to put my hair up in a ponytail and now have a sudden craving for a milkshake."

They laughed, both of them happy with the decision that had been made although Tarmin wondered if their relationship would stagnate staying like it was or would it develop further into something more tangible that would see them spending the rest of their lives together. By his own admission Zac had had plenty of partners since Gail and just because she was the chosen one at the moment, well that didn't mean he felt any more for her than any of her predecessors. For all she knew she could be just another link in the chain. Love or commitment hadn't been mentioned by either of them. Her feelings, she knew, ran deep. He already knew she liked him, that she was deeply attracted to him, that darn question and answer thing had alerted him to that fact, but did he realise just how much? Would he shy away from her if she was to tell him that she would one day like to have children, possibly his children? They'd never discussed it. There hadn't been a need to discuss it so why was she thinking about it now?

She'd never encountered anyone like Zac. The words 'soul mate' sprang to mind and she immediately chastised herself for thinking it. Their physical relationship was nothing short of spectacular. He only had to touch her or look at her in a certain way and she was transported into a totally mindless fool. No one had ever affected her like this before. She wondered if she affected him in the same way.

She gazed at him, her face still showing the signs of her thoughts and was disconcerted to find that he was staring at her. "What," she asked colouring slightly. Had he been speaking to her and she hadn't heard because she'd been thinking about their possible future.

"I was saying that I want to get you a ring," he told her again watching her face for any reaction she might have to the idea.

"A ring, what sort of a ring," her heart had started pounding as she looked up into his eyes.

"A friendship ring. I remember my grandfather telling me that when he first started going out with gran he said he bought her a friendship ring. It meant their relationship was exclusive although it didn't always follow on that a couple progressed past that point for going steady could last a day, a week, a couple of months, whatever. Apparently you went steady with a variety of people, not at the same time mind you, before you found that one special person."

"Fascinating," she told him wondering if he'd imparted this particular story to her as a roundabout way of telling her that he wasn't really serious; that he didn't intend for their relationship to go beyond its present perimeters. Maybe he was just having some fun. Did he have a trail of friendship rings scattered around the countryside? She wondered if Gail had worn a friendship ring. Somehow she couldn't see her as the kind of woman who would agree to such a frivolous arrangement. It would have to be a wedding ring or nothing. Zac had told her she'd been nice, but how nice was nice? His judgment had been clouded by love while your judgment is clouded by jealousy.

Perhaps I should tell him how I truly feel. It would be better to end it now if he wasn't serious. This was the precise reason why she hadn't wanted to get involved with Zac Coghlan; why she should have said no to going out with him in the first place. She thought as relationships went it had disaster written all over it.

She'd gone out with Kelvin for two years, but in the end he hadn't cared enough to make a lifelong commitment to her but within the space of a few months he knew he loved her sister, Carrie, enough to want to marry her. They were still deliriously happy according to her mother who kept her updated at Tarmin's insistence. At least now she could finally say she was truly happy for them and start trying to find her own happiness.

———————

Despite being so vehement about not wanting to go out Tarmin had to admit to feeling a certain amount of excited anticipation about her forthcoming dinner date with Zac. She decided she was going to dress to kill and chose from her wardrobe a provocative little number that she knew would knock his socks off.

The dress was black with a deep plunging neckline that showed her breasts off to perfection before falling away softly to encase her slim figure within a soft envelope of swirling chiffon. Tarmin loved it. It was reminiscent of the dress styles of the forties. She'd had it especially made after falling in love with the design after having seen it worn in one of the classic movies that she so loved to watch.

Her accessories included a pair of black leather sandals which had four inch stiletto heels and a small slim black clutch handbag that had been made to accompany her dress. Her jewellery was a matched set; a pendent necklace, made from beautiful black opals, fell between her cleavage drawing the eye to her full, rich breasts. There was also a bracelet, drop earrings, a ring and two hair clasps to complete the set. Her jewellery had been hand made by her grandfather and had been passed down through her mother's family line ever since.

She chose to wear her hair pulled back from her face and small wisps were teased out and fell in soft curls from her temples. Opal clasps held the rest in place before it was allowed to fall freely cascading around her shoulders.

Tarmin studied her reflection in her bedroom mirror turning this way and that trying to make sure that everything sat just right. She'd taken time with her make-up wanting it to be flawless. Satisfied with her appearance she had just applied a final coat of lip-gloss when she heard a knock at the front door.

"Zac," she said her heart racing. She hoped he appreciated the extra effort she'd taken tonight, for it had all been for him.

Standing for a few seconds behind the unopened door Tarmin took a few deep breaths to steady her nerves. She hadn't seen Zac since leaving work this afternoon. He'd informed her he'd be picking her up at seven pm and he'd be using the front door.

Opening the door to him she stood looking out at him before saying simply, "Hello, Zac, do you want to come in before we go?"

Zac stood motionless staring down at her before he finally found his voice. "You're absolutely beautiful, Tarmin, you look stunning."

He swallowed needing to clear his throat before he could speak again. "I got you these." He handed her a dozen red roses hardly able to drag his eyes away from this beautiful vision of womanhood who stood so enticingly before him.

She was perfect in every way. He reached out to tenderly touch her cheek with fingertips that trembled slightly. He was filled with a raw, primitive need that shook him to the core. He could feel himself becoming aroused and had to fight the mounting desire spiraling deep within his body. He tried to school his thoughts away from the vision he saw of Tarmin writhing beneath him while they made passionate love and breathing in deeply, he fought to overcome his constant appetite for her.

"So I take it I pass muster, Mr. Coghlan?" she asked him feeling satisfied with his response.

He slowly nodded his head as he moved further into the entranceway. "As you knew you would."

"I wanted to please you," she explained to him simply.

"Please me, don't ever think you have to please me, but I'll tell you something, Ms. Blain, something that I'm sure you already know, every man in the restaurant worth his salt will be drooling into his soup after feasting his eyes on you tonight."

It amazed Tarmin to think of how easily she and Zac always found something to talk about. Sometimes it was utter nonsense that was sprouted and would have them roaring with laughter or they could go to the other extreme and become embroiled in a deep debate over world issues, but not once did Zac berate her if her opinion differed from his own. He respected her right to have her say. She also cherished the times when just being together, sitting quietly side by side, was the order of the day. Tonight they were indulging in small talk and as they sat waiting for their meal. Tarmin was explaining to him the origin of the jewellery she was wearing.

"I was told by my mother that he found them," she was telling him, "He was making his way to the gem fields near Walgett," Zac raised his eyebrows in an inquiry.

"Walgett, it's in New South Wales. Anyway, he came across a corpse . . . true," she said seeing Zac's expression of disbelief.

"Down by a billabong," he tossed in for good measure.

"Do you want to hear this story or not?" she declared giving him the evil eye.

"Of course," he stated adamantly.

"Then stop interrupting," she told him menacingly.

"Okay, sorry," he murmured contritely sounding totally insincere.

She sent him a warning look as she continued, "Right, as I was saying before I was so rudely interrupted, he came across a corpse and being a decent sort of fellow he buried him," Zac pursed his lips wanting to add the billabong jibe again but he wisely said nothing letting her continue.

Tarmin eyed him suspiciously, but kept telling her tale. "He had a swag which my grandfather opened hoping it would contain a name, an address, but there was nothing except these black opals. Years later when he met my grandmother he had them made up or made them himself. I'm not really sure on that point. Anyway, he gave them to her as a wedding present."

"I'm sure they looked as lovely on her then as they do on her granddaughter now," Zac told her looking at the splendour of the brilliantly coloured opals resting against her creamy white skin and sitting so alluringly within the deep valley created by her breasts enticing his gaze ever downwards.

———

"I have something for you." They had just finished eating a most delicious meal. Zac had booked a table at Paulina's; an elegant restaurant situated in the heart of the city. He'd deliberately chosen a place where he wasn't known; he didn't want any awkward reminders of other times or people coming up to them to spoil their evening. He wanted this night to be special for all of the right reasons.

Raising her eyebrows inquiringly Tarmin wondered what he was up to; her heart had started pounding as she recalled their conversation from the other day. She realised she was holding her breath as she looked across at him.

He was fishing for something from within his jacket pocket and after what seemed to be an eternity he placed a small velvet box on the table between them.

"Is that what I think it is?" She wanted confirmation. A slow smile had started to spread across her face and she realised she was filled with a heady excitement as she waited for him to open the box.

"Open it and find out," he told her softly as he slid the box further across the space between them.

"Aren't you the one who's supposed to open it?"

"Okay let's open it together," Zac had to admit to a certain amount of excitement himself. This was a momentous occasion for him as well. He had never, ever, since Gail had a relationship go so far that he wanted to buy a ring. Actually his feelings for Tarmin far exceeded anything he'd felt for any other woman including Gail. Now he saw the giving of this ring to Tarmin as the continuance of something truly spectacular. He hoped she viewed it in the same light; as a beginning of things to come.

With trembling fingers Tarmin flipped the lid back while Zac held the box in place. She took a quick intake of breath when her eyes fell on the beautiful diamond encrusted ring laying within the satiny folds of the case.

Her eyes flew to his face and she lifted trembling fingers to her lips as she told him brokenly, "Zac, it's beautiful." Unanswered questions were tumbling through her mind. When had he found the time to purchase her ring? Why hadn't he taken her with him?

"I was hoping you'd like the choice I made." He'd agonised over the choice he'd made for there had been so many designs to choose from, but he'd kept coming back to this particular ring with its wide band and small scalloped edges. The diamonds were small but they took up every available bit of space on the surface of the ring.

Smiling happily across at her as she took the ring from its box he waited until she'd removed the opal ring from her finger before carefully sliding his ring onto her finger. It fitted perfectly as he'd known it would. He'd bought a wedding band wishing that it was going to be used for its traditional purpose.

"How did you know my ring size?" she asked as she gazed down at the ring which glittered so brilliantly on the third finger of her right hand.

"I borrowed one of your rings where you left it laying on the bathroom bench," he informed her taking another ring from his pocket to lay it in the palm of his hand to show her.

She hadn't even missed it.

"Are you ready to go," he asked her a short time later glancing across at her wanting conformation. Images of holding her; of making love to her kept intruding into his thoughts and it was becoming harder to concentrate on anything else.

"More than ready." Her words held a sweet promise of things to come.

More than one male glanced at her running their eyes appreciatively over the soft curves of her hips and the supple fullness of her breasts following her progress as they made their way through the array of tables towards the front door of the restaurant. Zac watched with a small smile playing around his lips while guiding her with his hand; he felt like turning around and telling them to stop staring for she belonged to him.

"Did you see that?" he asked her as they settled themselves into his car.

"No, what?"

"Remember what I said about every male in the place drooling over you . . . ," at her look of pure ignorance he nodded back towards the restaurant then added with a grin, "as we speak they're handing out extra napkins."

She smiled at him. "I think you're exaggerating just the tiniest bit. Anyway, there's just one person I want drooling over me."

"Mission accomplished," he stated sending her a dimpled grin.

"Zac," she conceded turning in her seat to tell him, "I enjoyed myself tonight."

"So did I, so if I wanted to take you out again you wouldn't be adverse to the idea and make me bring you kicking and screaming?"

"I guess not," she shrugged indifferently.

"That's hardly a yes," he intimated pinning her with a blue eyed stare.

Tarmin gave him a wry glance wanting to know. "Have you changed your mind about staying at home now that we're going steady?" Going steady, how strange that sounded to her ears, "you're not going to get all bossy now, are you?" She was hard put to keep the laughter at bay as she related this last piece of information to him. She'd bet everything she owned in the world that Zac would stay exactly like Zac.

"Takes too much effort," he answered while turning the key in the ignition and began to negotiate the twists and turns through the maze of cars in the overcrowded car park, "but if taking you out means seeing you in that outfit again . . . ," he briefly took his eyes from the road to throw a scorching look her way, "well . . . ," he swallowed taking everything in, Tarmin sitting there in that mind blowing dress, the sexiness she exuded just seemed to completely overpower his senses and heaving a deep sigh he continued, "You test a man's limits sitting there looking so damn sexy in that damn dress."

Chuckling softly in the darkness Tarmin smiled across at him. "This old thing," she crooned baiting him outrageously while bringing her fingers to the nape of her neck and wantonly started to drag them down over her breasts ever so slowly to finally rest demurely in her lap.

"Do that once more and we won't make it home in one piece." He told her brokenly as he fought against his emotions which were telling him to stop the car and take her right here on the side of the road.

"Okay, sorry," she murmured contritely sounding completely insincere.

Payback, he smiled thinking she could have timed it a bit better.

The drive back to Tarmin's place was completed in record time. *Thank goodness there were no police around,* Zac thought, *or I'd be in possession of a speeding ticket.*

Once inside Zac immediately took Tarmin into his arms. She responded in kind. "You, my lovely Tarmin, have been torturing me all night." He pulled her firmly against his hardened body drawing a ragged breath as his body registered the soft suppleness of her against him.

"See if we'd been at home there wouldn't be all this urgency," she tossed at him before he extinguished all coherent thought from her mind. The bantering was replaced with a deep sigh of satisfaction as she lost herself in Zac's powerful embrace.

His wild kisses, held in check for so long, spilled out along her jaw line covering her face, her neck anywhere his lips could reach until in exasperation he willfully picked her up in his arms and marched purposefully towards the bedroom where he gently lay her down on the bed before sitting down to join her.

Gazing up at him through passion glazed eyes Tarmin welcomed him. With shaking hands Zac undressed her, kissing each place where there had been clothing scorching his way downwards until Tarmin was writhing uncontrollably beneath him.

"Zac . . . please . . . if you have . . . ," she fought for breath, "any mercy . . . please . . . please . . . take me now," Tarmin begged. Euphoric tears were streaming down her cheeks and she unconsciously buried her teeth into him while trying to stop the tide of passion from unleashing itself too soon.

"I'm here, Sweetheart . . . I'm here," Zac's breath was ragged and he'd been hard pressed to answer needing to take a great gulp of air into his lungs to enable him to utter those few words.

He entered her then and Tarmin immediately wrapped her legs around him anchoring him more securely against her fevered body. Sliding easily into her silken softness he was received with a joyous, excited squeal that immediately sent their bodies into turbulent motion as they were both catapulted into a frenzied whirlpool of seething emotion until they lay completely spent, both drenched in sweat, but oh so very much sated.

Later that night as Tarmin lay quietly sleeping nestled contentedly in the crook of his arm Zac told her softly, "Tarmin Elizabeth Blain, I love you."

A stony silence greeted his words as he'd known it would, but he felt strangely contented having uttered them. His only wish was that when he was ready for her to know his heart she'd say the words back to him. Turning slightly he placed a tender kiss on her cheek before he, too, fell into a dreamless sleep.

"Wake up, sleepyhead. Its time to get ready for work." Zac was holding a breakfast tray with coffee and toast for them both.

Tarmin was laying on her stomach and sleepily opened one bleary eye to look up at him. It was still dark outside. "Go away."

"Wake up on the wrong side of the gum tree, did we?" he inquired totally unperturbed by her outburst.

"I was having this lovely dream," she mumbled into her pillow.

"You can tell me about it while we eat."

Sending him a sheepish grin Tarmin said she'd rather not as she slowly manoeuvred herself into a sitting position to accept the coffee and toast he handed to her.

"Oh, one of those dreams," he intimated knowingly sending a dimpled grin her way, "don't tell me I didn't do my job properly."

"Aftershock," she confessed lightly knowing he'd understand, but she felt her face flood with colour none the less.

"Me too," he confessed letting her know she wasn't the only one who was still feeling the effects of last night.

Eating her toast Tarmin started to ponder a question that had been plaguing her since last night. Their clothes were piled up beside the bed, a telling testimony of their haste to be with each other. Turning towards him and biting her lip indecisively she asked, "Zac, you liked me in that dress I know, but do you like it when I'm wearing my daggy old clothes and stealing your t-shirts?" They'd discussed it before, she knew, but she had to ask again wanting to be sure.

"Especially then," he told her truthfully.

———

There was a light tapping at her door and Tarmin groaned inwardly as she readied herself to look up wondering who her visitor would be this time. There had been a steady stream of her co-workers coming in to say hi to her this morning. According to these people they just happened to be passing her office door and thought they'd call in to have a chat. News of her wearing Zac's ring had spread like wildfire through the office and she'd been the recipient of congratulatory calls ever since.

A group of workers had seen them talking to Laura and Bill in the car park. Zac had just broken the news to his relatives telling them they were going steady. They'd had to put up with a lot of good natured bantering about their official status, "Going steady, do people still do that?" Bill had asked them. Tarmin had been concerned but Zac had shrugged indifferently telling her not to worry that it would save them the trouble of making an official announcement. He'd gone on to say that by the time they stepped through the front door the whole place would be buzzing with the news. *Boy had he been right*, Tarmin thought, *for if one more person walked through that door to congratulate her she was going to scream.*

It wasn't that she didn't appreciate the sentiment and the well wishes for heaven knew she did it was just that everyone kept bringing up the subject of marriage asking her if they'd set a date. How could she tell them she didn't even know if Zac loved her let alone if he wanted to marry her? It was all starting to get the better of her and she could feel her spirits starting to flag with every new visitor she received who just happened to be passing her office.

"Can I come in?" a familiar voice asked.

"Guy," her face flushed with pleasure, at last a truly friendly face, "yes, please do and shut the door after you. With a bit of luck we won't be annoyed by anyone wanting to see my ring." Holding up her hand she waved it in the air for emphasis.

"You can't blame them. You're big news at the moment, my girl. You're the one who successfully toppled the most eligible bachelor in the place."

"I thought he didn't go out with anyone from here?" She'd hate it if any ghosts from Zac's past suddenly started to come out of the woodwork to haunt her newly found happiness.

"He hasn't which makes it even more newsworthy," he imparted to her before asking seriously, "This might sound like a silly question to ask at a time like this, Tarmin, but are you happy?" He'd noticed the strained expression on her face seconds before he'd entered the room, before she'd realised he was there.

Understanding that there was a deeper meaning behind the root of his casual inquiry Tarmin took her time in answering and when she did she said soberly, "I still don't know where we're headed, Guy. My feelings are so strong and while I know he cares for me this," she held her beringed hand out for him to see, wanting to further explain her point, "didn't come with any written guarantees that a marriage proposal would automatically follow."

She went on to tell him, "You have no idea how embarrassing it's been having to fob people off. I don't know the playing rules, Guy. Just about everyone in the place has been asking me about marriage. I don't have any answers for them. Hell, I don't have any for myself. It's only a friendship ring, after all." Tears sprang unbidden to her eyes and she brushed them away with the back of her hand embarrassed that he should see her cry. It was then that she remembered something one of the women had said to her and giving him a watery smile she related her tale to him, "Do you know Joanne?" at his nod of affirmation she continued, "She thought you and I were seeing each other and was quite concerned about your welfare when she first heard about Zac and me. Can you imagine that?"

"Well we do spend a lot of time together when I'm not traipsing around the countryside."

It was true, Tarmin thought they did see a lot of each other at work and when he wasn't they usually emailed each other. "But surely people don't think . . . ," Tarmin sent him a troubled look, "but you're my best friend. I love you to bits, only platonically of course. You're the big brother I never had."

"Of course."

"I'm not going to give you up as a friend, you know that, don't you?" she told him grimly as another wave of depression washed over her making her brush feebly at her eyes as fresh tears threatened to spill down her cheeks. She'd talk it over with Zac tonight. He'd know how to best advise her and together they'd tackle the problem sorting it out to its logical conclusion.

Guy's eyes narrowed and his expression became thoughtful as he looked at her. "I believe a bit of R and R is in order here. Can you get away for a couple of hours? I have some park business to take care of in Yeppoon then we can have some lunch. If you remember we never did get around to having our dinner date so you owe me one."

"Oh Guy," she told him thankfully, "that would be wonderful." Glancing at the pile of paperwork on her desk, she thought, *to hell with it*, "I'll just clear it with the boss first, okay, then I'll meet you in say . . . ," she checked her wristwatch, "ten minutes."

"Right you are," he agreed.

Spending this time with Guy would help to lift her spirits. She realised he was probably her best friend, her only friend here in Australia with whom she felt close enough to talk to about the concerns that were troubling her with the exception of Zac, she corrected herself as she walked briskly towards his office, but even though he meant everything to her this was one subject she was unable to broach with him.

Zac's office was empty, in fact there seemed to be nobody around at all who could be told that she was about to play hookey. Biting her lip indecisively she wondered what she should do. She didn't think Zac would mind, but she was still a park employee and as such he should be informed of her whereabouts especially since she was leaving the park. Giving his mobile a quick ring she was perplexed to hear the ring tone coming from his desk drawer.

"Great," she muttered in exasperation, "I'll just have to leave him a note." Walking around his desk she sat in his chair and caught the distinct aroma of his aftershave. She breathed in deeply loving the musky scent and the memory of him that it invoked in her.

Reaching for his message pad she noticed Brenda, his secretary, had already scribbled a note for him to read. Tarmin was taken aback when she realised the message was from Colleen. She wanted Zac to contact her as soon as possible. Colleen, the name rang a bell, now where had she heard her mentioned. Drumming her finger tips on Zac's desk she thought for a few seconds before it came to her that Colleen was the woman Zac had been seeing prior to having met her.

Don't jump to conclusions, she told herself sternly as her mind started to conjure up all sorts of images involving Zac and this woman. There is probably a valid reason for this. *Trust him, my girl, just trust him,* she told herself looking down at the ring he'd so recently placed onto her finger hoping that somehow it would quiten the fears that were starting to build up in the pit of her stomach.

Glancing at her wrist watch she saw her ten minutes were up and scribbled Zac a quick note telling him she was going to Yeppoon with Guy before racing out of the room not wanting to keep Guy waiting any longer than necessary. When signing her name she'd also drawn three little heart shaped icons hoping he'd appreciate the gesture and maybe give his thoughts a nudge in the right direction. She hoped she wouldn't be in trouble when she got back.

Guy's business for the park took all of ten minutes to complete after that the time was theirs to squander as they pleased.

CHAPTER EIGHT

||||||||||||||||||||||||||

Tarmin had to admit to having a wonderful time and it was midafternoon before they arrived back at the park "Well back to the real world," she told him sadly as they made their way back to their respective offices. On an impulse created out of a need to see Zac Tarmin changed direction and headed for Zac's office.

"Hello, Brenda, is Zac in?" she asked casually stopping by the other woman's desk hoping the conversation wasn't going to automatically turn to her and Zac.

Throwing her a startled look before whispering, "Where have you been? Zac's been looking for you."

"I left him a note earlier saying I was going out with Guy," Tarmin answered wondering why he hadn't received her message. "Can I go in?"

"If you're game. Better you than me," came the swift reply, "would you take these in for me. They require a signature." Brenda thrust the paperwork into her hands before rising from her chair saying she was going to get a much needed cup of coffee.

Wondering what was going on Tarmin walked into Zac's office. She found him sitting in his chair but it was swivelled away from his desk as he looked out through the large glass window that took up practically the whole of one wall giving the onlooker a magnificent view of the surrounding landscape.

Coming into Zac's office always impressed her. His office was large and occupied a corner of the building giving him a panoramic view of the outside world and set into the other wall there were sliding doors which opened out onto a balcony where patio furniture stood still waiting to be used.

Zac was looking out through the windows and the casual onlooker would be forgiven for thinking that he was enjoying the view when in fact he hadn't noticed any of it. His thoughts were focused squarely on Tarmin as he tried to fathom why she'd want to go anywhere with Guy today of all days.

"Zac," she said hoping he didn't mind being disturbed. She thought for a moment that he wasn't going to acknowledge her presence but then he turned to face her and she knew instantly that he was bothered about something. *His face looks so grim,* she thought, no wonder Brenda had been so reluctant to come in. "Had a bad day?" she asked coming further into the room. She felt guilty that her own day for the most part at least since escaping the park anyway had turned out so nicely. She'd been able once again to talk things over with her friend and had come to the conclusion that she was going to have to iron out some things with Zac before very much longer.

"You could say that," he told her somewhat shortly not appreciating the fact that she'd waltzed into his office as if nothing had happened. She just took off without a word . . . with Guy of all people he'd been informed by a

number of park personnel who'd seen her running out to the
car park to meet him. His pride hadn't allowed him to phone
her asking for an explanation and he'd spent a miserable day
closeted in his office in the guise of catching up on paperwork
wondering where she was and more importantly what was she
doing?

"I was out with Guy. I told you in the note I left," she told
him while scanning his desk for the errant piece of paper. Surely
he'd gotten her note. *That would explain the grim expression*, she
thought.

His desk was now covered with files and piles of paperwork
and her message was nowhere to be seen. "Honest, Zac, I did
leave you a note." Shifting a few of the files around she spied the
small piece of paper stuck to the back of another piece of paper.
Brenda must have placed the work on his desk without seeing
her massage. "There," she told him triumphantly pointing
towards it, "there it is."

Picking up the rumpled piece of paper Zac read what he
already knew . . . that she'd gone out with Guy preferring to
spend the day with another man instead of with him, but still
he had to know why and he intended to find out before she left
this room. He gazed up at her shrugging his shoulders as he
brought his hands up in an asking gesture while he waited for
an explanation.

Tarmin let out a long drawn out sigh before she plunged
into an explanation about why she'd left the park with Guy.
This wasn't how she'd expected him to greet her. *Sometimes
life can be so unfair*, she thought as she looked across at him.
He was upset that much she could tell. How could she tell
him she loved him when he was throwing daggers at her with

his eyes? "It just got too much for me to bear. Everyone was coming up to me offering me their congratulations . . . which was lovely," she added noticing his look of consternation, "but then they started asking when were we getting married?" Her bottom lip started to quiver and she was twisting her hands together nervously as she looked at him hoping he'd understand. This could be the shortest friendship ever if he asked for his ring back. "I didn't know what to say to them. Whatever I said would have been a lie," she finished lamely then added wanting him to know, "I did try to phone you, to tell you, but your mobile was in your drawer. I had to get away, Zac, I just had to."

"My mobile was on the charger. I forgot to recharge it last night. As for the other, well, people were asking me too. I told them we hadn't discussed it yet." As an explanation it had seemed simple to him. Why couldn't she have said the same?

"I've left the park before on business so why get so hot under the collar about it today?"

Because you went with bloody Guy, his mind screamed at her, but instead he told her, "I don't know. I think it would have been good to present a united front to everyone and you didn't exactly go out on business, did you?"

"You can always dock my pay," she threw at him aiming for a bit of joviality hoping this ridiculous situation would soon be resolved between them.

Knowing he wasn't going to win this particular discussion with her unless he was to state the true reason behind his dissatisfaction Zac decided to give in gracefully. He wasn't about to tell her that he minded that she was spending so much time with Guy. People lately, when he inquired as to her whereabouts would tell him, 'She's with Guy,' or 'I think I saw her in the cafeteria with Guy,' or 'Out in the park somewhere with Guy.' He was getting so that he didn't try to seek her out any longer preferring to stay in his office because he didn't want to see her in the other man's company. *Why couldn't she be like normal women,* he asked himself and seek out the company of other females who liked nothing better than to sit around and dissect relationships? That would be preferable to her spending so much time with Guy.

Making a snap decision he got to his feet and walking around his desk he didn't stop until he stood in front of her. Taking a deep breath and placing his hands squarely on her shoulders he uttered softly, "For what it's worth, Tarmin Elizabeth Blain, I happen to be very much in love with you."

Tarmin's face crumpled and tears filled her eyes as she gazed up at him. Her bottom lip trembled with unsuppressed emotion and lifting her fingers to his lips she gently caressed them with her fingertips before telling him, "I love you too." He kissed her then not caring if the whole world came barging through his office door.

The world seemed a happier place as Tarmin went about her duties for the rest of the day. She had a lot of work to catch up on, but she didn't seem to care that she was ensconced in her office behind her desk writing up reports. *Zac loved her,* her heart sang. *He loved her.*

"Are you planning to be much longer?"

Tarmin jumped in her chair then looked up at her visitor, her eyes wide with fright. She'd been so engrossed in her own little world that she hadn't heard Zac walk into her office.

"Oh, you gave me a fright," she told him catching her breath. "I want to get these reports finished before I leave then I can spend all day tomorrow outside." She glanced at the clock on her wall and was surprised to see how much time had elapsed since she'd come back into her office. It was time to leave.

Who with? Zac's throat itched with the effort it took not to ask that particular question. Instead he came further into the room and pushing her notes out of the way sat on the side of her desk. It no longer mattered who with did it not since she'd told him she loved him?

In one deft movement Tarmin wheeled her chair to the side and positioned herself between his dangling legs. She rested her elbows on his thighs and her hands cupped her face as she looked up at him.

"Are you finished for the day?" she wanted to know.

"Mmm. I have to see someone before going home though. How would you like to share a bottle of wine with me tonight?"

"That would be lovely," she purred up at him, "any special reason?"

"None that I can think of," he claimed throwing her a heartfelt smile, "except one."

"And that is?" Her heart had started to race thinking of the words she knew he was going to say to her for those same words were forming on her own lips.

"I love you," he told her bringing his lips down to cover hers in a soft lingering caress that had her pulses hammering for he was also stroking her nipples with his thumb and forefinger bringing them to taut attention under his expert guidance.

"That's not fair," she whispered against his mouth loving the delicious feelings his touch always initiated within her.

Of their own accord her hands had moved to his thighs inching slowly higher until they reached their desired destination and she started to gently massage him as he sat in front of her. His reaction was instantaneous and she felt him growing under her tender ministrations.

His hands left her breasts and he entwined his fingers in her hair as a pure guttural sound of longing was forced from his lungs. He squirmed under her touch wishing he could be free of the clothing that was keeping him just out of her reach.

Oh god, she was tugging at his belt, undoing it while she attacked his zipper freeing him so that he was completely exposed to her. She looked up at him bestowing him with a passion glazed look before slowly lowering her mouth lovingly over him.

———

Respectability had just been returned to Tarmin's office when they heard someone approaching down the hallway outside her office. Zac was still sitting on her desk and had just finished rearranging his clothes.

"Quick, move," Tarmin tried to push him away not wanting to be seen in this compromising position.

"It will look more suspicious if I move," he told her casually while taking a deep breath needing to bring his ragged breathing back to normal perimeters.

He hadn't meant for this to happen, but once she'd touched him he'd been lost. Release had been sweet and because of their surroundings somewhat quick for both of them had the notion in the back of their minds that they could be sprung.

Tarmin quickly propelled her chair backwards until she was propped up awkwardly against the wall. Zac was laughing softly at her as she tried to inject a note of respectability into the room.

Laura joined them a few minutes later. Walking into the room she casually dragged the only other chair around to their side of the table before sitting down to join them She lazily kicked her heels off and stretched her body out wanting to get rid of the tension of the day. "So what have you two been up to? I must say I'm completely stuffed."

Tarmin shuffled in her chair slightly embarrassed that they'd nearly been caught. She looked across at Zac who, in turn, sent her a knowing smile that had her face flaming a deep crimson hue. *You have no shame,* she thought self-consciously having to avert her eyes away from him.

Not waiting for an answer Laura launched into a conversation about the upcoming night at the Leagues Club. "It seems there is to be a Karaoke night. Some of the girls are placing bets on who will give the best performance." Tarmin's face flamed again. She really had to concentrate and stop thinking about a certain male of the species who was sending her senses haywire just by looking at her.

"Can you sing, Dear?" Laura wanted to know.

"Like an angel," Zac informed his aunt. She sang to him every night while in the throes of their love making. It was the sweetest sound he'd ever heard.

Stop it, she cautioned him her eyes flashing.

"Really," came the interested reply.

"No," Tarmin told Zac's aunt, "your nephew is pulling your leg." She sent him a menacing look that did nothing to quell the smile lingering on his lips or to send those delicious dimples back into storage at least for the time being.

Zac brought their conversation to a halt when he got to his feet saying to his aunt, "Come on, Aunt Laura, it's time we left Tarmin in peace. She wants to finish her notes before leaving tonight and I still have someone to see when I leave." Then turning to Tarmin he asked, "How long do you think you'll be?"

"About an hour should do it."

"Okay, would you like Chinese for tea? I don't feel like cooking tonight."

"You don't cook anyway. Stop bragging. Your aunt knows you too well," she responded laughingly.

Taking hold of his aunt's elbow he propelled her out of the door saying as he went, "Aunt Laura, let me tell you about this horrible woman I've become involved with. She's bossy, won't let me get away with anything . . . ," his voice receded into the distance as they walked further down the hallway and was followed by Laura's light burst of laughter.

Tarmin reluctantly turned back to her computer. She'd better get started if she was going to get this work done in time. She recalled Zac saying he had someone to see, *probably a client,* she thought wondering who had staked a claim on his time.

Finally finishing the last of her files Tarmin checked her e-mails to see if there was any from her parents. This had become a daily ritual; one she immensely enjoyed for it brought her family close to her for a few minutes every day giving her the chance to tell her parents about the day she'd had. She'd insisted before leaving America that her mother be connected to the net. It was so much more convenient than conventional letter writing in that it was instant.

Telling her parents about Zac had been difficult. She hadn't known exactly how to broach the subject to them. Her mother had been extremely happy that she'd found someone to love for she'd been worried knowing of the heart rending pain Tarmin had suffered, but successfully hidden from the rest of the family concerning Kelvin.

She'd even introduced Zac to her parents over the net. It had seemed so strange sitting in her office talking to her mum and dad using the web cam Zac had let her set up. There had been quite a few oohs and ahs from her mother when she told her laughingly that she and Zac were going steady. She'd been told later by her mother that she thought Zac was quite a dish.

Tonight the news was simple, not much to relate really. She told her mum they'd unveiled her friendship ring today saying their friendship had been met with much curiousity and an enormous mountain of questions concerning their ongoing relationship. She told her mum to stop worrying about her for she'd found the man of her dreams. She went on to tell her that there was to be a work gathering on Saturday night for the employees at a local sports club. It will give me a chance to get to know the people with whom I'm working a little better.

"This place really packs 'em in doesn't it," Tarmin said looking around her with interest at the different forms of entertainment as she entered the establishment with Zac. There were large television screens suspended from the ceilings so regardless of where you were sitting you could follow the sport of your choice be it football, soccer, dog racing or horse racing. There were also gambling facilities for those who were so inclined.

"It's a pretty popular haunt for a lot of the locals," Zac told her as he guided her towards the long trestle table which had been reserved for their private use. "It's got a bit of everything as you can see. Parents can bring their kids here to watch the footy and then have a meal as well if they choose to," He indicated out to the football field where a game was in progress.

"There's Laura," Tarmin said making her way through the crowd to sit down next to Zac's aunt. "Okay if we sit here."

"Yes I saved two seats for you, Dear," Laura told them as they greeted the other people already seated at the table.

Tarmin saw Guy sitting further down the table and waved a cheery hello to him which he instantly returned.

She turned to Zac saying, "I just want to have a word with Guy. I won't be a minute."

Zac watched her walking towards the other man and tried to still the gnawing sensation he felt in the pit of his stomach whenever he saw the two of them together. He was forced to turn away when his attention was claimed by another co-worker who had come over to talk to him. When he was able to look back Tarmin had disappeared.

Tarmin had excused herself from the table to go to the bathroom. "So are the two of you living together now?" Sarah, one of the park employees asked her as they both stood before the mirror in the ladies room running a brush through their hair.

"No we have our own houses," Tarmin answered simply but chose not to tell the other woman that they only lived a stone's throw away from each other, a mere slip through the hedge. *Although we spend every available minute in each other's company,* she thought contentedly. It struck her then that this is how Carrie and Kelvin must feel about each other for remembering back she recalled how often she'd found them together locked away somewhere in a world of their own making; one which had always excluded her.

"I think it's so romantic how the two of you found each other," Sarah was saying, "It's just like fate brought you together from opposite sides of the world."

Tarmin smiled knowing she wouldn't have explained it quite like that, but she agreed none the less.

"Can I have another look at your ring please, Tarmin?"

Holding out her hand Tarmin found herself in the centre of a group of women as a few more ladies from their group walked into the toilet block.

"Did you get it engraved with any special words?" one of the women asked her.

"Do you know I don't know," Tarmin admitted truthfully taking her ring off to look on the inside of the broad gold band. She wasn't going to go into how they'd been at a restaurant and he had simply placed the ring on her finger. Sure enough there was an inscription there which ran twice around the band which read, "Tarmin, I love you now and forever, Zac" There had even been room to inscribe two entwined hearts.

Tarmin was completely overwhelmed and scarcely heard the comments of the women around her as she took those words and placed them next to her heart.

On returning to the table she gave Zac a quick kiss on his lips and softly murmured for his ears alone, "I love you," which had everyone making catcalls in their direction. He raised quizzical eyebrows at her wondering what had prompted her show of affection.

"Just felt like it," she told him happily. She wasn't about to launch into a lengthy explanation about her feelings regarding the similarities between their relationship and her sister's or the fact that she'd discovered the message he'd had inscribed into her ring. She'd tell him later.

Tarmin found she was enjoying herself being here with her work collogues. They were a good bunch and good company to boot. She hadn't laughed so much in a long, long time. *Of course Zac played a major role in her overall happiness,* she thought contentedly looking at him. Shortly after they'd finished eating Zac asked her if she'd like to dance. The club sported a small dance floor and a few couples had already taken to the floor taking advantage of its use and were gyrating to the music provided by a live band.

As if they had been cued to do so the band started to play a slow song as soon as they walked onto the dance floor which brought Tarmin intimately into Zac's strong embrace.

"Ah, I like this," he crooned contentedly letting his body sway to the soft beat of the music. His hands were linked loosely around her waist while Tarmin's arms had crept up around his neck and her face was cushioned by the strength of his broad shoulder. She sighed contentedly closing her eyes letting the mood of the moment completely overtake her.

An announcement coming over the loudspeaker brought them back to reality. The Karaoke competition was about to start so anyone with a vested interested was to make their way to the bandstand to register.

"Come on," Tarmin said pulling Zac back to the table, "I want to listen to this, it should be a hoot." She went on to tell him how some of the park staff had told her they were going to compete.

Surprisingly some of the contestants weren't half bad Tarmin had to concede a short time later after having listened to a few of the singers. One girl in particular had a really good voice and had been given a standing ovation by the crowd. Tarmin had to smile indulgently when Zac pointed out to her that half of the audience was drunk and the other half would clap at anything.

"She is still good though," she told him appreciating the voice she was listening to.

A movement behind her had her looking around and smiling up into Guy's face, she asked what she could do for him.

"You can join me on stage. Marci conned me into doing a song with her, but she's chickened out so I need a partner. How about it? It's just a bit of harmless fun."

"Me," Tarmin wailed, "not on your life." She looked at Zac hoping he'd agree with her and although he had a strange look plastered across his face he said nothing to convince her she shouldn't do it.

"Zac, tell him I can't go. Exercise your rights as my boyfriend."

"Don't you dare, Zac Coghlan," a chorus of female voices filled their immediate vicinity lead by none other than his aunt who then added, "Go on, Tarmin. It's good fun."

"It seems I'm outvoted." Was all he said sending her a casual glance that she wasn't able to read, but she was sure that for a second there she'd seen his eyes flash with distinct disapproval.

Well I did try, she thought reluctantly as she was cheered onto the stage by several onlookers who were standing nearby.

"You'd better make it a song I know," she told Guy, then said to him under her breath, "You owe me big time for this, fella."

"Marci had this one picked out. Do you know it?"

Tarmin looked down at the piece of paper he held in his hands. "'Billy Gilman, I Wanna Get To Ya'. Yes, I know it, thank goodness. It was on the charts a few years ago in the States. Did you hear it out here?" She had nerves dancing in the pit of her stomach, in fact she thought they might be boot scootin'. This definitely wasn't her thing to get up in front of a crowd. She preferred to blend into the safety of the background being part of the audience. She felt acutely embarrassed and just wished the whole episode would come to an abrupt end so that she could skulk off the stage as quickly as possible. Also, she wasn't entirely sure why she thought it, but she had the idea that Zac wasn't happy about the idea of her being up here either. *Well she'd asked him to help her get out of it so he couldn't blame her*, she thought rebelliously looking down at him from where she stood on stage.

Their names were called out as the next contestants and amid a lot of good natured hooting and cheering from the floor she and Guy launched into the lyrics of their chosen song.

Tarmin immediately felt the effects of the adrenalin which had started to rush throughout her body and thought, *what the heck if I'm up here I may as well make the most of it and have a good time.* She played up to Guy swaying her jean clad body outrageously in unison with his and when she playfully made a play for his clothes actually undoing the top two buttons of his shirt he bared his chest and pulled her to him and as their duet finished they were treated to a wild raucous chorus of, "More, more, more."

Still caught up in the throes of the moment she placed her arm casually around Guy's waist and he did the same as they bowed outrageously to their audience. Guy placed a light kiss on her cheek before grabbing one of her hands to hold it up in a victorious gesture.

Guy and Tarmin won the competition hands down receiving a small trophy which Guy said she could keep for if it hadn't been for her outlandish behaviour they wouldn't have stood a hope in hell.

"You know what this means though, don't you?" he told her as they made their way back to where Zac was sitting waiting for her.

"No, what?" she wanted to know.

"We now have a trophy to defend,"

"Oh no you don't. I'm not doing that again anytime soon," she laughingly admitted to him, "Once is enough for this girl." It had been fun to be sure and she was still riding on a high burst of adrenalin that would take ages to leave her body, but she just wasn't interested.

"Okay I'll concede defeat and hand you back to Zac," Guy told her as he saw her back into her chair.

"What did you think of that?" she asked Zac showing him the small plastic trophy they'd been given. "I've never been so scared in my life."

"Really, it didn't show," was all he said. She'd looked good, damn good in fact and if it had been anyone other than Guy up there with her he'd have been full of praise for her efforts, but he thought, his jaw set in stone, *why did she have to include that little sexual byplay into the piece.*

It didn't help when one of Zac's friends piped up and said, "Watch out, Zac, or Guy will be stealing her away from you right under your nose."

Tarmin was stunned to see the grim reaction setting Zac's face into stone and not wanting an awkward silence she said, "No chance of that happening, Fred. I've got the man I want right here." She patted Zac's hand hoping this small gesture on her part would appease his spirits. Okay, she'd gone slightly overboard, but it had only been a bit of harmless fun surely he realised that.

She was rewarded with a slight smile and although it didn't quite reach his eyes she was satisfied that a small disaster had somehow been averted. She couldn't fathom why Zac would be annoyed with her, but she knew he was. Now wasn't the time or the place to talk about it, but when they got back to her place she was going to have it out with him.

After suffering a stony silence from Zac that she couldn't seem to penetrate or understand Tarmin grabbed her bag and told him offhandedly, "I'm going to play the pokies for a while."

Sitting dejectedly in front of a poker machine while absently feeding it coins Tarmin's thoughts kept straying back to Zac and his unnatural behaviour and she wondered what she could do to make things right between them. She just couldn't work it out and then it hit her like a bolt from out of the blue, he was jealous; the stupid man was jealous of Guy. Everything slotted into place and she heaved a huge sigh of relief.

She jumped when a hand tapped her on the shoulder and turned to look up into Guy's sombre face. "Hey you." She acknowledged him sadly.

"I've come to apologise for your case of the blues. It seems I've put my foot into it by asking you to help me out back there." Guy told her reaching out to push a stray lock of her hair back into place behind her ear. He'd noticed Zac's withdrawal since he'd done the Karaoke number with Tarmin and when she'd left the table, he'd followed her.

"Is it that obvious?" Tarmin wanted to know placing her hand over his as he touched her face, "but, you know, I think I've figured it out." She launched into her explanation of Zac's churlish behaviour.

"You know I think you may be right," Guy agreed then added, "I'll go and have a chat with him and straighten everything out, okay."

"We can both go because you know what they say . . . there's safety in numbers." She laughed then happy that this whole silly business regarding Guy was about to be cleared up once and for all. She didn't want to lose his friendship or Zac's love over a silly misunderstanding.

Their plan was thwarted when they saw Zac approaching them. His displeasure was evident. His face held an anger Tarmin had never seen before. She'd been holding Guy's hand letting him guide her out of the poker machine area.

"Zac, we were just coming to see you," Tarmin told him lightly trying not to be frightened by the haunted look he was sending her.

"I have to go. I'm sure Guy can see you home," he flung at her before turning on his heel to stride away from her heading towards the door.

Swallowing hard Tarmin could feel the tears gathering in her eyes as she looked up into Guy's face.

"Stupid man, stupid, stupid man," she whimpered brokenly as she folded herself into Guy's strong embrace no longer able to hold back her tears.

Upon reaching the door Zac looked back not able to help himself. His fists clenched into hard balls as he saw Tarmin being taken into Guy's arms. He felt like someone had reached into his very soul and ripped his heart from out of his chest, the pain he felt was so intense. He'd been on his way to find Tarmin wanting to apologise for his boorish behaviour. He'd been prepared to eat crow regarding his attitude towards her obvious friendship with Guy when he'd seen them together. It was obvious they were enjoying each other's company. All thoughts of giving an apology disappeared to be replaced with an overwhelming desire to smash Guy's face in. He filled his lungs with a deep shuddering breath while trying to quell the menacing thoughts his own personal greed eyed monster was conjuring up in his mind. The best thing he could do for Tarmin at this point in time was to put some distance between them so that he could clear his mind and try to think clearly. Perhaps then the solution to this fiasco might come to him.

"That went well," Guy said trying to inject some humour into the situation. "Your theory about jealousy rearing its ugly head seems to have some merit."

"Shut up," Tarmin said hitting his chest with her fist, "This isn't funny. Can't he see how much I love him? I don't know what else to do," she confessed miserably.

"I don't think anyone would be convinced of your love for him at the moment," Guy reasoned and at her look of confusion added, "look where you are. Standing in another man's arms being held romantically for all they know."

"But," Tarmin racked her brains trying to come up with a plausible excuse if asked why she was in Guy's embrace.

"Come on," he told her gently, "I'm taking you home and together we'll wait for Zac to return so that all can be explained."

"I don't deserve you," she told him simply letting him lead her away towards the door that Zac had so recently used to vacate the club.

"Quite possibly," he agreed glibly.

Zac had literally walked the streets for hours trying to rid himself of his demons before jumping into his car to drive up to Mount Archer where he spent some more time working through his feelings for Tarmin. He was nursing a bruised ego and he knew without a doubt that the only person who would be able to assuage his hurt feelings would be Tarmin herself; that is if she was prepared to listen to his ramblings. She'd told him she loved him and in his heart he knew she meant it, but he hadn't been prepared for that very public display up on the stage tonight. When Guy had gone down on his knees sliding across the stage stopping only centimeters away from Tarmin's thigh singing, 'I Wanna Get To Ya' he'd completely lost the plot. *Who wouldn't*, he told himself trying to summarise his erratic behaviour with a valid excuse but none came readily to mind. Words like fool, idiot, loser and moron flowed quite freely through his thoughts however as he realised how stupid he'd been. He'd found the perfect woman, the one he wanted to spend the rest of his life with doing all of those mundane activities that married couples engaged in like buying groceries, doing the washing, helping with the housework and where was he, sitting in his car in a lonely mountain top car park sulking and feeling sorry for himself when he really wanted to be with Tarmin kissing her, loving her, asking her to marry him.

This decision made he turned the key in the ignition and the powerful engine sprang to life taking him back to the only person in the world who meant everything to him.

———

"Would you like some more coffee?" Tarmin asked Guy as they sat and waited hopefully for Zac to return.

Shaking his head Guy said no. They'd been home for a few hours now and Zac still hadn't showed up. At Tarmin's insistence he'd put his car in her garage for as she pointed out if Zac saw it he might jump to the wrong conclusions all over again. She was certain that once he had time to sort things out in his mind he'd see how silly he'd been to react so strongly.

Her head was starting to ache and she was worried that she was going to go down with a migraine of shattering proportions before this whole mess could be cleared up. *Stupid, stupid man,* she said to herself gritting her teeth as the pain in her head started to increase. If she took medication she'd be out for the count so she had to hold on a bit longer.

"Guy, I'm going to have to lay down or my brain is going to explode out of the top of my head." She explained to him starting to stand up but lost her balance as a wave of nausea assaulted her.

"Okay, that's it off to bed; No more waiting," he gathered her up into his arms and carried her through to the bedroom and was in the process of laying her down onto the bed when Zac burst into the room.

"What the hell is going on here," he stated taking in the scene he imagined was being played out before him. He failed to notice Tarmin's pallor or the pain that was etched into her face. All he could see before him was treachery and deceit. They'd played him for a fool. If he'd been a few minutes later he would have caught them in the act.

Tarmin lifted trembling fingers to her lips hoping she'd be able to explain what was happening wanting to stop the tirade of words that she knew was about to come tumbling out of Zac's mouth before he started to speak for she knew they'd be fanned by anger and misunderstanding. The words would be scathing in their intensity but they would also be wrong.

"Don't," she pleaded beseechingly, "I know how this must look, but nothing has happened here. You don't realise how wrong you are."

Dragging an unsteady hand through hair that was already unruly Zac looked down at her wanting to believe her, but facts were facts. He'd practically caught them in the act. As long as he lived he'd never be able to erase the image imprinted on his mind of seeing Tarmin being carried in to bed by Guy. Never in his life had he wanted to attack someone so badly; never had he felt so much hostility towards another person. He felt his hands bunching up into fists as he looked across at the man who until recently he'd always looked on as a friend.

"To think I was actually going to give you the benefit of the doubt," he spat at her before turning on his heel to retreat from the room. He wouldn't give them the satisfaction of seeing how badly affected he was by the scene he'd just witnessed.

Tarmin's migraine kicked into high gear then with the pain shooting through her head becoming so acute from the added burden of stress Zac's outburst had caused her to bear.

"Please, Guy, go after him," she pleaded thickly, "bring him back." She tried to raise herself up onto elbows that were too weak to hold her weight but failed miserably and fell back against her pillows banging her head which had black pin points of pain flying haphazardly before her eyes forcing her to shut them tightly as another wave of nausea assaulted her.

Guy sprang into action. He'd chase Zac later making him understand if it killed the both of them but first he had to get some medication into Tarmin.

"Take these," he said a few minutes later standing over her with water and two pills.

"Won't work now," she said gritting her teeth as another wave of pain shot through her head.

"Take them anyway," he persisted, "they might help you to sleep."

———

Falling into a troubled sleep Tarmin awoke to a room that had been artificially darkened. The blinds had been pulled down and the curtains were drawn so that the outside world had been successfully obliterated. She groaned moving her head and was instantly greeted with a sharp pain that struck her squarely behind the eyes making her wince.

She thought she'd been alone, but someone's hand covered hers soothingly, gently massaging her palm. "Zac," she asked feebly, "Is that you?"

"Yes, Sweetheart, go back to sleep. I'll still be here when you wake up later."

"Zac," she wanted to talk but comforted by the soothing sound of his voice and the gentle touch of his hand she was lulled back to sleep.

———

Opening her eyes, Tarmin looked around the room. She was thankful that she felt free of the mind blowing pain she had endured. Her head still felt heavy but she knew the worst was over.

"Zac?" was he still here or had she been dreaming he was here with her.

"I'm here," he answered quietly.

"I thought I'd dreamed you up," she told him feebly turning her head to look at him. "What time is it?"

"Eight-thirty," he told her then added as an afterthought, "Monday night."

"What. How did I sleep for so long?" *Nearly forty eight hours,* her mind calculated.

"I kept giving you your pills and they kept you sedated."

"How did you know to do that," she wanted to know.

"I rang your mother asking her what I should do," he explained and had simply followed the instructions he'd been given. She hadn't woken, just swallowed the pills and kept sleeping.

"Zac, why are you here?" Although it probably seemed a silly question to ask she had to know.

"Because I happen to love you," he told her simply.

"About Guy," she broached the subject carefully not certain what had happened while she'd been out to it.

"We had enough of a talk for him to convince me that he wasn't interested in you; that he was here because you were waiting for me and then your migraine struck so he was helping you into bed," but there were still areas of gray as far as he was concerned. Questions he had to have answered.

"Is that all he said," she pressed him for more information.

"He said you'd fill in the gaps when you were able, but it seems to me that a bloke would have to be gay not to want to make love to you."

"Exactly," Tarmin agreed. A slow smile converted her features into a wonderful grin as she watched the transformation taking place on Zac's startled face as the truth of what he'd been told fully hit him.

"Get outta here, not Guy!" he exclaimed.

"Yes, we have only ever been friends, Zac."

"But," he faltered momentarily at a loss for words, "but he's had girlfriends."

"No, Zac, he hasn't," she corrected him, "he's had girl friends." At his look of total confusion she explained further, saying, "Friends who are female. There is a subtle difference. Now do you understand?"

Total silence followed for a few seconds as Zac's mind processed this new information. It was mind boggling, earth shattering, in fact.

"So," he asked her thinking it through as he spoke, "you're telling me he wasn't . . . didn't at any time have the hots for you. He's never wanted to sleep with you? He hasn't . . . you weren't . . . ," he was falling over his words as he tried to take in the knowledge that Guy was gay.

"No," she thought wisely that now wasn't the time to tell him that Guy thought him attractive and had it not been for the fact that Guy knew he was heterosexual he'd have asked him out.

"Can we put all of this behind us, please, not forgotten, just behind us?" he asked her simply as he took her into his arms to hold her gently against the length of him mindful of the fact that she was still unwell.

"Tell me something," Tarmin asked wanting to know if her suspicions were correct.

Zac waited for her question.

"Did you send Guy away on those business trips on purpose; on some wild goose chase because you thought he might be interested in me?"

Zac had the grace to look a little shame faced. "I would have sent him to the moon if it meant getting him out of the way," she was told confirming her suspicions.

"What am I going to do with you," she asked him breathlessly for he had started to nibble on her ear forgetting momentarily about her headache.

"Marry me," he told her matter-of-factly, "that will stop me jumping to mistaken conclusions about you and your friend."

The look she shot at him was one of pure indulgence.

"You know what I mean."

"Yes I know what you mean," she agreed happily.

His voice changed to a low seductive whisper. Gone was his flippant attitude of before. "I love you," he stated simply, "Do you understand what I'm saying, Tarmin. I love you so much."

"Yes," she answered him softly, "I understand perfectly. I love you too."

"I want the lot. House, kids, mortgage . . . the lot," he imparted to her.

"Stretch marks," she threw in casually.

"Those too," he agreed, "I think I'm man enough to handle those as well."

Bracing herself up on one elbow she asked, "So," cocking her head to the side pretending to be thinking about the words she was about to say, "it's okay if I kiss Guy like this," she kissed him chastely on the cheek, "but I'm never, ever, to do this, or this?" She moved her hand slowly up his thigh until she was touching him intimately on his groin. She had the satisfaction of feeling him spring to vibrant life under her hand and then bringing her lips down to cover his she wantonly massaged his lips with her tongue before delving it deep into his mouth then withdrew it to tell him, "Okay, I think I've got it sorted out now."

"Good," he moaned knowing he was about to lose total control of the situation. "I'd hate to think we were on different wave lengths. Are you well enough for this?" God, he hoped so for he wanted her so badly he was aching.

"Let's see shall we," she invited, offering him her lips.

PROLOGUE

"Come on, my little flame thrower, come to Daddy," Zac's arms were outstretched and a tiny replica of Tarmin launched herself into his arms while screaming excitedly, "Daddy, daddy."

"You have a baby brother," he told her proudly while hugging his three year old daughter warmly to his chest. He hadn't thought it was possible for one heart to hold so much love and still have room for more.

"How is Tarmin?" Laura wanted to know standing quietly in the background watching father and daughter as they greeted each other. Zac had dropped Alana off at Laura's on the way to the hospital promising he'd let the both of them know immediately when Tarmin had given birth to their second child.

"Excellent. The Doctor reckons she's a natural. It looks like we have another redhead in the family though." Zac beamed up at his aunt. The birth of his children still filled him with wonder. He remembered how awe struck he'd felt when he'd been asked to cut Alana's umbilical cord. It was a moment in time he'd never forget. His heart had swelled with unconditional love as minutes later he'd looked down awe struck into the face of his daughter as she lay nestled in her mother's arms. Now it had happened again and those same feelings had resurfaced to completely overpower his senses.

His family meant everything in the world to him and at that moment Zac felt that he was the luckiest man alive. He had a beautiful wife, his soul mate, whom he loved and adored utterly and completely. Now they had two beautiful children born out of the love they had for each other. His life was complete; it could only improve, getting forever better.

THE END